THERE'S SOMETH

The young airman arrived ~~at~~ ~~Fifty-four~~ in the predawn hours of a Sunday. He was startled to see the shape of a crew member sitting in the navigator's seat of the B-52. The officer was in the shadow but it looked like he was doing some paperwork . . . in almost total darkness. The airman just stood on the hatch steps in confusion, trying to let his eyes adjust to the gloom. The shape turned toward him and reached for the helmet in his hand. As it moved into the dim light from the hatch, the airman was horrified to see that the body ended above the shoulders. He could clearly see the lieutenant's bars on the flight suit, but there was no head!

* * * * *

It is the position of the air force that things such as ghosts and goblins do not exist. They have no basis in fact and are therefore not officially recognized. It is also a fact that from that day on, even with the ramp as crowded as it was, the air force never again used Charlie Fifty-four as a parking space for a B-52.

AND IT WILL TAKE YOU WITH IT—INSIDE THE PAGES OF . . .
SCAREFORCE

✈

"An entertaining revelation of the determination of 'warriors' to stand their watch, beyond the duration of life itself."

—Richard Marcinko, bestselling author of *Rogue Warrior*

SCARE FORCE

Maj. CHARLES D. HOUGH, U.S.A.F. (Ret.)

WARNER BOOKS

A Time Warner Company

WARNER BOOKS EDITION

Copyright © 1995 by Charles D. Hough
All rights reserved.

Cover design by Mike Stromberg
Background photo by J. Warden/Superstock

Warner Books, Inc.
1271 Avenue of the Americas
New York, NY 10020

 A Time Warner Company

Printed in the United States of America

First Printing: November, 1995

10 9 8 7 6 5 4 3 2 1

This book is dedicated to my father . . .
who wouldn't have believed a word of it.

SCARE
FORCE

PREFACE

THE United States Air Force is made up of men and women who are intelligent, professional, well trained, capable, and haunted.

I don't mean to say that every single one of the 400,000-odd blue-suiters has his or her own personal specter to keep them company. But if you can get them talking, if you can gain their confidence, if you can become a friend, then you might hear strange tales and fantastic stories that stretch the imagination.

The military profession is unique. So are the people who live the life. They're given the best training, armed with the most advanced technology, and then pushed out to the edge to do impossible things.

After twenty-five years of association with the Air Force I've learned that strange things happen out there on the edge. When the people and their machines are pushed to the limit, all that pressure sometimes leads to surprising experiences.

I'm not a trained parapsychologist or professional investigator of the paranormal. I don't know where the things that go bump in the night come from. I've heard conjecture that violent death creates ghosts. The Air Force provides its fair share of that. The first aircraft fatality was a member of the military. Lt. Thomas E. Selfridge died in a plane crash in 1908 while a member of a unit that evolved into the modern Air Force. And men and women of the Air Force have been dying in tragic ways ever since.

But whether these specters are formed by violence or pain or fear or something entirely different, I know they're out there.

The stories that follow are from my own experience and the experience of my friends. Some of the names have been changed. Some of the places are different. But they're all stories of the Air Force with a supernatural chill. Enjoy.

THE ALERT PHANTOM

*I*T was hard to lose friends to flying accidents, especially during peacetime training missions. But then again this wasn't really peacetime. The cold war generated situations like Alert and dangerous training missions. Alert is gone now, and the missions are easier. But as you'll see in the following story, all of the cold warriors haven't been relieved of duty.

"On Alert again. Looks like they got me on Alert again." Captain Gavin chuckled as the young gunner passed him, paraphrasing a popular country ballad. Some of the humor wore off as he considered his own situation. On Alert again. Alert was a necessary evil that helped to maintain the precarious balance of superpowers in the midst of a prolonged cold war. Here young men and women, the cream of the crop of modern day warriors, were gathered on the threshold of Armageddon. They were pilots and crew chiefs, navigators and bombardiers and munitions specialists. Together with their modern engine of war, the huge B-52 bomber, they lived on the edge of the sword for seven days at a time. High, razor-topped fences, motion detectors, vicious guard dogs, and a heavily armed security force kept them separated and protected from the normal world of the Air Force base. Protected also from family and friends. Nothing must distract them from their task. They had to be always ready. They were as isolated as if they were already in a war on foreign soil.

Captain Gavin felt that he had spent too many seven-day weeks poised on the sword's edge. Being ready day and night to jump into the mighty bomber and fly in the teeth of the most dreadful of battles was a young man's game. The way he saw it, four of his last twelve years had been spent in this Alert building prison.

Not that it was all that uncomfortable, as prisons go. The building was like a two-story, totally self-contained hotel. It had its own kitchen and dining room to serve up to a hundred warriors. It had a library, a well-appointed game room full of the latest video games, a couple of television lounges, and even a modern movie theater. It had its own fleet of vehicles maintained by its own service station; the old-fashioned kind that really provided service. It had a full suite of offices for the personnel who maintained this most exclusive of hotels, and a communications network that would have been the envy of most multinational companies. The living quarters were private and well furnished. The fact that the lower story was buried underground was only a little ominous. It was no more strange than the total lack of windows anywhere in the building. An attempt had been made to alleviate the gloom through the use of brightly colored walls and an eclectic collection of paintings. It was a vain attempt to relieve the air of doom from this final outpost on the road to nuclear holocaust.

The tension of Captain Gavin's situation and his surroundings no longer had a serious effect on him. After twelve years he felt only a little of the terror of his situation. What did cause fear and trembling in him was the thought of his desk creaking under a terrible load of paperwork. Paperwork that was mostly overdue. And it looked like it was going to remain overdue for at least another week. All Alert personnel were restricted to the building because of problems with the Klaxons. The Klaxons were noisy horns located everywhere on the air base. Their banshee wail would summon the warriors to their planes when the time for war was called. When they weren't working, nobody left the building.

Dale Gavin sighed as he paced down the long main hall. He felt restless and uneasy. Here he was isolated from a mountain of work. He guessed he should be grateful for the rest. All he really felt was boredom. When he had been a new young warrior, Alert was exciting. The shared adversity drew the crews together in a camaraderie that was intense yet hard to describe to an outsider. Crews were like a strange, six-way marriage. They worked as a unit and they suffered or triumphed together.

Now he wasn't really a member of all this. He was the outsider. He was a staff officer drafted to fill a vacancy left by a vacationing navigator. He had already played all the crew games and had been elevated to a different realm; an executive, if you will. He was considered an "old head" by the crew dogs now. A reservoir of corporate knowledge. A seasoned veteran. "Yeah," he thought. "Old fart is more like it."

Old Captain Gavin glanced up as the door at the end of the hallway swung open. He smiled as he recognized another "old head." It was Mike Delane, a longtime friend. They had started out in the command together, attending the same flying class. They had been to war together and survived the danger of conflict and the boredom of Alert. Now they both served on the staff that administered the bomber wing, teaching old tricks to new dogs.

Mike came sauntering up the hallway with the easy stride of a man confident enough to take it easy. Dale noticed the ubiquitous coffee cup in his friend's hand. Mike never seemed to be without it. He was looking down at the ground as he came, as if trying to remember the punch line to an old joke or another war story. The younger flyers had been known to ply him with free beer after long flights to loosen his memories of the outrageous youth of the command.

"See they caught you too," Captain Gavin said as his friend drew near. "Guess they'll let just about anybody defend the nation."

Mike must have heard him. The corridor was quiet and empty except for the two. But he didn't look up or acknowledge the greeting. He just plodded on.

Dale was confused. Maybe Mike had a lot on his mind. He was about to repeat the greeting when Delane drew even with him. Mike looked up; gazed steadily at Dale. Then he smiled slightly and winked. At that moment a cold breeze blew down the hall. Gavin turned to the side to see who had opened one of the flight line doors. He turned back to comment on the strange chill to Mike only to discover that the hallway was empty. Quickly he examined all the doors that led off the hallway. All were closed. It was as if Mike Delane had disappeared into thin air.

"Very funny." Gavin spoke to the empty corridor. "Aren't you a little old to be playing hide-and-seek, Mike?" The last was delivered with more conviction than he felt. He was aroused from his confusion by the loudspeaker on the wall above him.

"Captain Gavin, you're wanted on the phone. Emergency!"

Dale forgot his missing friend as he sprinted down the hall to the communications room.

"Get your keys and be in front of the facility in five minutes. I need some crew training files, now!"

The wing commander's voice rang in his ears as he headed to his room to retrieve his keys. Gooseflesh ran up his arms. A demand for crew files like this usually meant only one thing in the flying business: an accident.

Dale's worst fears were realized by the commander.

"We lost one. About an hour ago. In Sand Fork. They landed right on top of the target."

Sand Fork was a training route that the bombers used to practice low-level bombing. The bomb run was in a valley between mountains in Colorado. It was a desolate area that looked like the surface of a dead moon.

"Were there any survivors?" It was a hard question for Gavin to ask.

"No chance." The answer even harder for the colonel.

The news was horrifying. Six men, fellow flyers, were now gone completely from the earth.

"Give me the folders for Jamie Bar's crew."

Now the dead men had names. Captain Gavin reluctantly pulled the training folders for the crew. They would be needed by the accident board, who had already been notified and would be convening rapidly. The Air Force moved quickly in situations of crises.

The colonel watched over his shoulder as he pulled the manilla folders from the cabinet.

"Not the nav. Not the lieutenant. He had a cold. The flight surgeon grounded him. They were flying with a substitute."

The colonel reached past him and pulled another folder from the drawer. Captain Gavin froze as he read the name on the folder. The blood rushed from his face and his mouth gaped open.

"It . . . it can't be . . . " he stammered.

"Here, Dale, you better sit down." The commander helped him to a chair. "I'm sorry I didn't break it to you a little better. I forgot that you guys were good friends."

Yes, good friends. Friends in adversity. Friends on Alert. But one of them was probably on a lot longer tour. Much longer than seven days.

Dale Gavin looked back at the name on the folder. The name of his friend, Mike Delane. For whatever reason the ghost of his recently deceased crew mate had returned to haunt the place that he haunted so often in life.

Sleep tight tonight, America. Your Alert Force is awake. But not all of us are alive.

NANNY'S GHOST

*T*RADITION *defines England as one of the most
haunted countries in the world. Steeped in history,
the stately ghosts of England are admired and respected as professionals in the realm of the supernatural.
Just as England perseveres, so do her haunts. But there's a
difference here that I think is important. Even though their
days and nights in the old manor house were full of strange
and supernatural occurrences, I never met a single partici-
pant who would have given up the experience. They seemed
to actually cherish being haunted by ghosts like these.*

Greenham Common is an unusual name for a United
States Air Force base. That's probably because technically
it's not a United States air base. It's a British base on loan to
the US military near the town of Newberry in the southern

part of England. It lies in a beautiful section of Merry Old and is a prized assignment.

When Air Force members change bases and move their families to new locations, especially locations overseas, the service tries to make the move as painless as possible. One of the facilities they employ to take some of the difficulty out of a move is the provision of temporary living quarters or TLQs on the base. They're like little motels furnished with most of the comforts of home. Servicemen can move their families in while they arrange for more permanent quarters either on or off the base.

Greenham Common was no different in this respect. But the TLQ itself was different. In fact it was probably the most "different" building ever used by the Air Force. Buildings were limited on the base proper. The USAF had looked around for a building to use off base and what they found was unusual to say the least.

Greenham Common TLQ was in fact a centuries-old manor house in the grand tradition of English nobility. It was still owned by the ancestral heirs of the builders and was leased to the government for the slight sum of one dollar per year. The only provision of the lease was that the Air Force do its best to preserve the manor house exactly as it had been given to them. No remodeling was to be done. It had already been modernized with plumbing, electricity, and heating before it was put into government service. The family could no longer afford to maintain so grand a dwelling.

And grand it was. It was three stories of antique beauty. The entryway was dominated by a bold staircase that swept up the entire three stories. Opposite the staircase was the entrance to the ballroom, a truly magnificent room. It occupied one-half of the entire structure, with a vaulted ceiling rising three stories above the marble floor. On one side of the room were two mezzanine levels leading off to multiple rooms. At another corner was an alcove housing an organ that seemed to float a story above the dance floor. At the end of this grand salon was a massive fireplace that easily accommodated logs eight feet long. People occupying the rooms off the ballroom could watch the activities below from the railing or join them by way of the enormous staircase. Other rooms led off the other side of the staircase. It was in all respects the most commodious and elegant building ever used by the Air Force. And it was probably one of the most haunted.

The manor certainly had enough provenance of age to allow for a host of phantoms. The building as it stood was some three hundred years old. In spite of this it was referred to as the new manor house. It was built on the ashes of an older house that had burned long before the United States got itself united.

Operating as it did as a temporary lodging facility, the stately TLQ did not house long-term residents who could build up a history of the ghostly happenings. But the Air Force is a close-knit family, especially in a foreign country. When family members got together for recreation, a favorite topic of discussion was the supernatural occurrences in the TLQ.

The most-commonly shared experience was the nightly footsteps of the busiest ghost. Many had heard the comings and goings late at night. The rooms were located on long narrow hallways with wooden floors. The ghost who walked there was not furtive or shy at all. He or she was bold and purposeful, even if no one living could determine what the purpose was.

A young sergeant recalled encountering the ghostly walker several times. He had a job that required him to work late hours. Returning to the manor house after dark, he usually sat up reading before retiring. The utter silence of the house would suddenly be disturbed by footsteps proceeding down the hallway. The steps were sharp and clear and he could tell that the walker was definitely a no-nonsense person. There was an almost-military precision to the staccato taps. No, it was more than military. It was a walk that demanded immediate attention. A walk like that feared and respected by most English boys. In other words, it sounded for all the world like the walk of a nanny. A nanny bent on ensuring that the rules, her rules, were adhered to straightaway.

This first night, as on many nights to follow, the footsteps came to a halt at his door. They were followed immediately by a sharp rap. The young sergeant, accustomed to reacting without question to authority, jumped to his feet and ran to the door. He was dumbfounded to find nobody in the hallway. In fact no other light showed from under any door in the corridor. He searched the hallway but could find no reason for the disturbance. He returned to his room and sat down to read again. In a few short minutes the walk and the knock were reenacted, with the same results.

On subsequent nights when the sergeant returned to his quarters late and stayed up to read or listen to music, the ghostly walk and knock were repeated. He could never find the culprit. He mentioned it to other tenants of the TLQ, but they just laughed and said that he must have done something to make the ghost mad. Their sleep had not been disturbed.

Finally one night, as the ritual was repeated and the loud knock was echoing down the hall, he said out loud, "Okay, alright, I'm going to bed." He did, and the footsteps were not repeated. From then on he found that if he didn't stay up too late, the ghost would leave him alone. It was almost as if he were being cared for by a nanny who wanted him to get his rest and would brook no disagreement.

In another room in the TLQ, at another time, a couple brought a young baby with them. The child was ill and cried a good deal of the night. The mother had to be up most of the night almost every night. She could look forward to only short minutes of sleep broken by the crying of her child. Her husband had to have his sleep to be able to work and the mother would not disturb him. But the nightly routine was having a serious effect on the mother's health. One night she fell into bed exhausted, looking forward to only a few precious minutes of sleep. She woke with a start and was amazed to see that she had slept undisturbed for several hours. Even more amazing was the lack of any sound coming from the child's room. Suddenly she was worried that something might have happened to her baby. She rushed to his room, but stopped short at the door. By the glow from the night-light she could see a form bending over the child's crib. The form was indistinct but had the appearance of a woman looking at the child with some concern. She seemed to be patting the child gently on his back. The baby was making small sounds of contentment. The mother watched for several minutes until she became aware that the shape had faded completely away. She returned to bed and completed her first full night of sleep in many days, entirely confident that her infant was perfectly safe.

One of the most amazing supernatural occurrences in the manor house took place in broad daylight in front of a large group of people. The base had planned an outing for the newly arrived service members and their families. They were taking a tour bus to a seaside resort and several families were hurrying to join the trip. A little three-year-old girl was at the head of a group coming down the grand staircase. Disobeying her mother's caution not to run, she was in full flight. As she rounded the last landing her flight became literal. Several shocked people watched in horror as the little girl tripped on the rug and launched herself headfirst into the air. Disaster seemed unavoidable. A woman screamed. Suddenly her headlong flight to certain injury or even death was arrested. It was as if she had been caught under the arms by an adult with amazingly quick reflexes. She hovered in midair and then, before a dozen bewildered and astonished observers, she was lowered gently to the ground. She skipped off to the bus as if nothing had happened, leaving in her wake a lot of speechless witnesses.

No one knows what ghost or ghosts haunt the old manor. But all of them know what kind of ghosts they are. The best. By all accounts, the very best.

SCARY MOVIES

A military base is a strange thing. Part-city, part-neighborhood, it gives you a sense of place like no other locale I have ever experienced. The facts of the following story always added a little extra thrill to watching scary movies at one particular base theater. I have used the name of a base that no longer exists, but the real base and the real theater are still in operation. Maybe you'll find them both some dark and stormy night.

Modern military bases are a lot like cities. Most everyone knows that they have housing, offices, and places to store a lot of military hardware. Some people who deal with the military know that there are a few other facilities of the type that you'd associate with a city. Things like service stations, municipal utility offices, and a police force. But you have to be in the military for a while to get to know how much like a city a base really is.

Few outsiders know that the military provides several types and classes of housing—everything from motels, to unmarried personnel apartments, to duplexes, to family homes, to luxury suites fit for a king . . . or a president.

Bases usually provide all the services you'd find in a comparably sized town. Everything from grocery stores to department stores, swimming pools to dry cleaners, hospitals to mortuaries. They can supply you with food, drink, clothing, furniture, reading glasses, automobiles, recreation, fun, and excitement. And, like any small town, a military base can sometimes provide you with the unusual, the strange, and the supernatural. You see, the bases are communities of people, both living and dead. Just like any town full of people, the dead sometimes come back to make life more interesting for the living.

Just about every base in existence has a base theater of some sort. The base theater usually serves as a multipurpose auditorium, furnishing a meeting place for commanders to brief their troops; a forum for visiting dignitaries to meet the base population; a large classroom for mandatory training sessions; even a stage for little theater groups. In spite of all this activity, they still get around to showing movies.

The theater on Kinchloe Air Force Base was no exception. It was being, and always had been, heavily used day and night since its construction more than a decade ago. And, as the new theater manager learned, it was also being used after hours for a purpose that the designers had not intended. For the theater at Kinchloe was home and playground to a ghost.

Staff Sergeant James Reynard was a professional weapons system specialist. He'd had a wealth of experience in his field and was considered resident expert. Levelheaded and rational, he was the last person you would expect to believe in something as unscientific as ghosts and hauntings.

But Sergeant Jim learned about the realm of the supernatural quickly after taking the part-time job of base theater manager. He had been on the job for a few months before he noticed the unusual occurrences. They started mildly enough. Several times theater patrons had complained about someone moving around behind the screen during the showing of films. They said that they could hear the footsteps and see the curtains on the side of the screen move and shake. And during quiet times in the films they would sometimes hear laughter coming not from the audience but from behind the screen.

Jim was reluctant to take the complaints seriously. He thought that they must be mistaken. The sounds probably emanated from somewhere in the audience. The moving draperies were just caused by errant breezes circulated as people came and went from the theater. The area behind the stage could be reached only from a single door at the back of the building or from the stairs leading up out of the audience seating area. After the complaints the back door was always found to be securely locked. And certainly no one had entered from the house. Jim himself acted as usher during the showing of films whenever he could and he had never seen anyone attempt to climb the stairs and go back in the wings.

As the complaints increased, he kept a more vigilant eye on the premovie activities in the house. It was during one of these nights, as he was watching the house fill up for a film, that he witnessed an occurrence that convinced him that something strange was responsible for the disturbances. While surveying the audience, he glanced up at the stage. He was astonished to see the curtain on the side lift up and continue up until it was at least five feet off the ground. It was if someone standing behind had lifted it up to get a look at the arriving audience. But anyone lifting the curtain like that would be in full view to everyone out front. There was no one behind the curtain.

Jim seemed to have been the only one to notice the curtain move, or at least the only one to understand that it was impossible. He signaled to the projectionist to hold the start of the movie for a few minutes and proceeded to search the area behind the screen thoroughly. He found the door locked and the area behind the screen totally empty of any living thing.

On another occasion, Jim had been advised by the environmental health office that a sister theater on another base had been severely reprimanded by the inspector general for all manner of candy, gum, and old popcorn found under the stage. The garbage had been thrown there by hyperactive children and was drawing in mice and rats from the neighboring fields.

Jim hired a young airman to clean under the stage. The area was reached by way of a small door set in the center of the stage and usually nailed shut. Jim was in the office of the closed theater catching up on some paperwork while his part-time janitor cleaned.

After about half an hour, Jim heard the doors from the audience area bang open. He was surprised to hear a loud, "I quit!" from his new worker. The airman didn't stop to explain. He just left by the front door as rapidly as possible.

Jim ran into the young man later that evening in the recreation center. It took a large pizza and couple of beers before he would tell Jim what had precipitated his hasty departure.

He said that he was under the stage, deeply engaged in

scraping out the antique residue from the snack bar. He had a trouble light with him but he had moved a few feet away from it. As he reached forward for a handful of trash, his hands passed through a cold area. It was shocking enough for him to draw his hands back. Suddenly, from right next to his ear, he heard a loud voice say, "Get out of here!" The voice sounded very angry, but there was no one with him in the crawl space. He left so rapidly that he didn't notice until later that he had received several scratches and bruises in his haste to leave. He displayed the injuries to the sergeant. Jim was not able to convince him to return to the theater. Jim ended up cleaning the area himself, without incident.

The most recent happening in the theater, and one of the strangest, took place on another late night after the theater had closed. Jim was in his office, finishing up some paperwork. His office was a tiny alcove, just big enough for a desk and chair. He was concentrating on some figures when, out of the corner of his eye, he caught a glimpse of movement. "It was as if someone had poked his head in the door, bent over, and glanced around at me," he said. "At first it looked normal and didn't really register. It was only after it had happened that I realized that he couldn't have poked his head in the door to my left: the door was to my right." The visitor Jim had seen would have had to poke his head through a solid wall. Jim concluded that he had done enough work for that night and quickly closed the theater.

There are many reasons why a theater on a base might be haunted. Young men and women entering the military are often sent far from home. They're forced to be grown-ups almost overnight and they're isolated from friends, family, and, on some bases, even from the local town. It's natural for them to gravitate to a place like a theater. It's cheap, fun entertainment and a great place for meeting others of their age. They go on to different assignments and too often to war and an early death. They may carry with them fond memories of the base theater. Maybe some are even drawn back after their time on this earth has passed.

Whatever their reason for being there, Jim continues to run the theater the best he can for all the patrons. He did add that the motion picture *Ghostbusters* was an enormous hit. Professional appreciation? Who knows?

TRANSATLANTIC GHOST

*Y*OU *can argue the relative merits of divisions, regi-*
ments, and brigades, but any military member knows
that the strongest unit in the Air Force is the family.
Without families, few could handle the pain and suffering of
a military career. True military families understand the sac-
rifices necessary to keep the country strong. As the following
story demonstrates, family love transcends the normal
boundaries of time and space . . . and life.

In the old days the military was not a place to be if you
were a family man or woman. The top sergeant used to be-
rate those so inclined with the adage, "If the Air Force
wanted you to have a wife, it would've issued you one!"
That attitude has happily died away with the advent of the
modern Air Force that "wants to join you."

Business learned long ago that a happily married worker is a stable and loyal worker. It just took the military a couple of hundred years to get the idea. Now, convinced of the value of the military family, they go out of their way to accommodate families. But even with all their good intentions, the reality of military life sometimes places great hardships on families.

The Freemans were such a family. Ted, the father, was a respected and professional sergeant. He was an electronics specialist, a profession in demand virtually everywhere in the Air Force. His wife, Vikki, was a teacher and a new mother. Their son, Teddy, was barely seven months old and already the favorite of numerous uncles, aunts, cousins, and grandparents.

Ted had spent an arduous three years working at a stateside base getting a new system on-line and running. His hard work had been rewarded with a plum assignment.

Lakenheath was a US military base in Suffolk County, England. It was in a beautiful part of Great Britain, not far from London. It was the kind of assignment that young families like the Freemans dreamed of. Even the form used to request assignment to the base was jokingly referred to as a "dream sheet." It was everything that they wanted. And it couldn't have come at a worse time.

The Freemans' assignment arrived in the same week that Vikki learned her father was afflicted with a particularly ravaging form of cancer. He was indeed dying from it. There was no hope. And there was no accurate way to determine how long he had left to live.

The minute Ted found out about his father-in-law's illness, he wanted to cancel the assignment. He was ready to apply for a humanitarian reassignment, one of the finer inventions of the military. He wanted Vikki to be with her father during the trying times to come.

Vikki's father wouldn't hear of it. Being a former soldier, he understood the value of an assignment like this.

"You take your family to England. It will be an experience you'll never forget. It'll help your career. And you never know, I just might decide to hang around regardless of what the doctors say."

Ted knew his father-in-law was right. To ease the pain of separation he arranged to take a long leave before departing for England. They spent as much time as they could with Vikki's father.

During the final week of their vacation, Vikki was gratified to see that her infant son had formed a very close attachment to her father. When her father sat down to read or talk, Teddy was content to sit beside him. At mealtime he wanted to be where he could see his grandfather. At night he wouldn't go to sleep unless grandpa said good-night. It was a precocious fixation but a pleasant one for Vikki and her father.

Time for moving came much too quickly, but Vikki's father did his best to make it a happy time. He hid the pain of his illness with amazing success. When the Freeman family left for England they were almost convinced that her father would be waiting for them when they returned.

England and the assignment were everything that the Freemans could have wanted and more. The job was perfect for Ted. He excelled at his work and his supervisors were appreciative of his talents and expertise.

The family moved into a rented cottage in a little town some distance from the base. They found the people friendly and the countryside beautiful. It was almost an idyllic time.

Little Teddy thrived on the brisk English weather. He was growing and changing every day. He was a happy child who continued to demonstrate a precocity beyond his young age. Everything seemed perfect.

Then one day about two months after their arrival at Lakenheath something happened. Teddy woke up in the morning crying. This was highly unusual for their normally happy child. He cried continuously. Nothing would quiet him. He was not hungry and would not eat. He didn't need to be changed and showed no interest in his toys. Being held and walked and cuddled by either parent had no effect.

Ted was reluctant to go to work and leave his wife with the child in such a state. Vikki insisted that it was a passing phase brought on by a nightmare or maybe the beginning of a minor illness. She insisted that Ted go to work. She could handle it.

But as noon approached with the child still crying, she was not as sure of her ability to cope. When Ted called and learned that Teddy was still upset, he directed Vikki to take him to the emergency room of the clinic immediately.

Ted met Vikki at the clinic just as the doctor called her name. The young pediatrician checked the child over thoroughly and pronounced him healthy. There was no physical reason for his distress.

He asked if Teddy had been severely frightened recently or if he had been separated from a favorite friend or toy. The negative answer left him as perplexed as the parents. He told them to take the child home and he gave them a prescription for a mild sedative that would help Teddy sleep.

The prescription quieted the child somewhat, but he did not fall asleep. His crying diminished to a sad whimper. His grief was almost unbearable in one so young.

His mother finally fell into exhausted sleep after the baby quieted, but Ted stayed awake, checking on the child every half hour. It was just after one of these checks that he lay back on the bed to try to get some much-needed rest. As he lay there wide-awake, his hearing tuned to the slightest change in his young son's distress, a strange thing happened. He clearly heard the living room door open and someone walk across the room. He jumped out of bed and grabbed the nearest thing that could be considered a weapon. It was a bullwhip he had purchased as a souvenir of a recent trip to Spain. So armed, he crept to the bedroom door. He listened as the footsteps came up the stairs. They were slow and measured, but definitely determined. As they reached the landing outside the bedroom door, Ted wrenched the door open and leapt to confront the intruder.

There was no one there. The hallway and, for that matter, the rest of the house was empty except for the Freemans. And the front door that he had heard open was still securely locked.

After searching the house for the third time, Ted was sitting in the living room. He was holding his son, who had overcome the effects of the medicine and was crying as he had all day. At that moment two things happened at once. There was a knock on the front door. Ted jumped up, startled, and headed for the door. Then he stopped, amazed. For at the exact moment that the silence was broken by the knock, Teddy stopped crying. He looked into his father's eyes and smiled. Then he closed his own eyes and fell fast asleep.

Ted stumbled to the door in a daze. The visitor turned out to be his first sergeant, the senior administrator for his squadron. He was surprised to see Ted up at this hour, but the sight of the infant in his arms alleviated some of the surprise.

"I'm sorry to have to bring you some bad news," the sergeant said. "I thought it best to come in person. I didn't want to tell you over the phone. I'm afraid your father-in-law passed away tonight."

Vikki gasped at the sad news. She was standing in the doorway to the living room, obviously wakened by the knock.

The sergeant left after ascertaining that there was nothing further he could do to help. He told Ted to make arrangements through the squadron for an emergency leave when he was able to come in.

Saddened by the loss of her father, Vikki was still shocked by the events of the previous night. The recounted story of the ghostly visitor was one thing, but the actions of their baby added immeasurably to the strangeness of the situation. It was almost as if the child had been mourning the impending death of his grandfather. And when it finally happened, he relaxed. It was as if Vikki's father had visited to say that everything was all right and Teddy was the only one to receive the message.

But the next day something even stranger occurred. It was something that removed all doubt, at least for the Freemans. Vikki was settling her son in his stroller to take advantage of the mild weather. She was in the hallway getting ready to go out the front door. As she straightened up she noticed a shadow on the wall behind the stroller. At first she thought it was her own shadow, but she glanced behind her to see that there was no light source to make the shadow. She looked back at the wall and watched the shadow turn so as to present a profile. The profile was immediately recognizable to her. It was definitely her father. She glanced down at her infant son and saw that he was smiling broadly at the shadow. She watched it and, as it gradually faded away, she was overcome with a feeling not of dread but of peace. She knew in her heart that her father had come to say good-bye. His ghost had crossed the ocean to assure her that it was all right.

DEATH REACHES OUT

*T*HE *following story is an example of how to hide in plain sight. The facts were right there in the headlines for all to see. But few civilians were able to read between the lines. It's also true that few Air Force flyers were able to overlook the irony hidden in the facts. Everyone of us has watched comrades go down in flames and wondered "Why him? Why not me?" And the only answer is, "must not be my time . . . yet."*

Predestination is a warrior's creed. The belief that your time for leaving this earth and this life has already been decided is a powerful tool for one who must face death every day. History's greatest warriors have held the belief and have prospered because of it. Stonewall Jackson knew that he could do nothing to avoid his death when it came for him.

Battle held no fear for him. He stood in the midst of shot and shell as though he were a stone wall. His courage inspired courage in his men.

Patton also knew that he had nothing to fear from battle. He knew he could not escape fate and did not try. In the modern military the belief is not so universally held. In the age of modern warfare, of computer chip aircraft and intelligent munitions, it's hard to believe in something as ancient as fate. But sometimes fate reaches out, through all the modern defenses and cybernetic soldiers, and once again its icy grip is felt.

The B-52 Stratofortress and the KC-135 Stratotanker were the heart and soul of the Strategic Air Command. They were the backbone of the nuclear defense of the United States and were a major factor in the winning of our longest war: the cold war.

To see these two giant aircraft engaged in the aerial ballet called midair refueling was truly awe-inspiring. Unfortunately, because it took place five to six miles straight up, it was a sight that few Americans were privileged to witness. The precise timing and almost superhuman control required to fly these behemoths of the air in connected flight, while hurtling through space at hundreds of miles per hour, was astounding.

The powers in charge of the Strategic Air Command in 1983 knew this. They also know that if a way could be found to demonstrate this dangerous ballet to the public, it would boost the image of the men and women of SAC. For years audiences at military and civilian airfields had thrilled to the aerial demonstrations of teams of fighter aircraft like the Blue Angels and the Thunderbirds. They were in such demand that their shows were booked months and even years in advance. They never failed to draw a crowd. And the reverence that the American public held for the pilots carried over to the rest of the military personnel assigned to their bases and commands. The young men and women who worked long, difficult hours to keep them flying deserved recognition. It was great for morale and great for public relations.

The SAC leaders knew all this and finally devised a plan to demonstrate the capabilities of their aircraft to the public. A "Thunder Bomber/Thunder Tanker" team was formed to demonstrate low-level air refueling. The team was comprised of the best bomber and tanker crews. They were given ample time and resources to develop a show-stopping display.

Only integral crews were used and they practiced for endless hours to perfect the show. They did most of their work at the northwestern SAC base where the crews were permanently stationed. They worked slowly but deliberately to produce the desired results with maximum safety. They went over and over each separate part of their routine to achieve perfection. Every crew member knew he was an important part of the team. Each knew what to do and when to do it. The navigator teams on both aircraft coordinated to achieve split-second timing. The pilot teams practiced precise and minute control. Every move must be anticipated and perfected. The tanker crew had to know exactly what the bomber crew was going to do and vice versa. The gunner and boomer operator were responsible for keeping exact separation of the two aircraft. All the crew members learned to act like the fingers of one hand. The demonstration was going to be perfect. Then fate stepped in.

On this day, the thirteenth day of the month, a series of maneuvers were to be rehearsed over the airfield. They were maneuvers that had been done before but that needed more polishing. The bomber was to flyby and then the tanker would do the same. After the simple flyby, both aircraft would move into position for a join-up and a pass of the viewing area in refueling formation. For the sake of realism a vacant lot that adjoined the runway at midfield was chosen to be the viewing area. It was easy to pick out from the air because it was the only vacant lot on the base side of the runway. It was flanked by the squadron building and an operations building and the far side formed the parking lot for the group of commercial shops known as the Base Exchange. The field was known to be a good place to watch the air show practice. A road that ran down the east side of the field was usually full of cars, but this day the road was almost empty.

It was a normal busy workday for squadron personnel, but they were able to look up from their desks through the windows on the west end of the building for a clear view of the demonstration area. Mission-planning crews enjoyed watching the practice and critiquing the abilities of their fellow fliers. This form of friendly harassment was endured by the elite crews chosen for the demonstration teams. It kept them from getting too proud.

On this particular day the crew study rooms were full of working airmen. But one of the watchers had nothing to do. Nothing that is except to fret and worry about his crew. He was the boom operator of the Thunder Tanker and should have been taxiing out to the runway. But the young sergeant was unable to be with them. He had come down with a cold and the Flight Surgeon, the flyers' personal physician, had designated him DNIF, Duty-Not-Involving-Flying for the next couple of days. It was not his fault that he couldn't be there with his crew. But he fretted just the same. He finally got in his car and drove out to the field to watch. He waved as the tanker with his crew and a substitute boomer taxied by for takeoff.

As the sergeant sat in his car watching the two aircraft make multiple passes by the imaginary viewing stand he noticed a jogger on the road by the vacant lot. He recognized him as a pilot from his squadron and waved to him. Personal fitness was a must for the aviators and nearly everyone in the squadron engaged in jogging.

The young boomer returned his attention to the aircraft floating above the field. Then at approximately one-thirteen, or thirteen-thirteen in military time, something happened.

The mission planners in the squadron were slow to realize what was happening. One captain finally recognized that something was gravely wrong. The tanker was descending much too rapidly and sideslipping directly toward the squadron building. He finally broke his paralysis and yelled for the rest of the crews to run. They reacted immediately and scrambled for the far side of the building.

The jogger on the road stopped to rest, glanced back at the runway, and suddenly found himself in an actual race. A race with death. For the tanker, a military version of the venerable Boeing 707, was coming directly at him. He ran faster and harder than he had ever run in his life.

Workers in the operations building across the field from the squadron were mesmerized by the sight of the mighty tanker, so completely out of control and rolling lazily on its side. Panic spread as they became aware that the aircraft would certainly land on their building.

People returning from shopping or just arriving to shop in the BX stopped in disbelieving silence as they watched the silver aircraft making directly for them. It was most assuredly out of control. Confusion was on every face. It was almost impossible to understand what was happening to the tanker. There was no immediate panic. Some even walked a few steps closer to the flight line to get a better look.

Everyone who saw the aircraft in the final moments of flight knew that a crash, a horrible crash, was inevitable. And they also knew in some primitive part of their beings that more than the crew would die in the wreckage. There was only one small open area near the runway. Only the little field. There was simply no way that the tumbling, careening aircraft could miss hitting at least one building.

Flying airplanes is an inherently dangerous business and flying military aircraft is the most dangerous of the dangerous. The Air Force is a closely knit family, drawn together by adversity. When something as terrible as an aircraft accident happens, a well-managed support system swings into action almost immediately. When a husband, wife, son, or daughter is struck down in the course of duty, word of that disaster must come from a fellow member of the military family. Friends of the crew members spread out to give the sorrowful news and be there to help manage the grief.

The base knew almost immediately that a KC-135 had crashed. Every wife who had a husband and every child who had a father that flew tankers waited in dread to hear. Who had it been? Who bought the farm? Who wouldn't be coming back tonight?

The wife of the boom operator, the regular member of the crew, felt a deep sorrow for the families of the other crew members. They were like her family. But she also couldn't help feeling a secret relief, knowing that her husband was safe. He had been saved by a little cold, such a minor thing to owe your life to.

She prepared to go to the squadron to see what help she could offer the survivors, the families of the missing men. As she started to leave the building she was surprised to see a friend coming up her walk with the squadron operations officer and the base chaplain flanking her. She was a little amused. They must have made a mistake. Her husband hadn't been on that aircraft. He was safe.

The crash was horrendous, instantly transforming the jet into twisted rubble. The JP-4 fuel in the tanks, enough to keep the aircraft airborne for several hours, ignited immediately on impact. The sound was a deafening roar. The impact was truly astonishing. And the wreck was astonishing in another aspect. Because, as impossible as it seemed, the aircraft missed the squadron building. It missed the operations building. It missed the Base Exchange buildings. In fact it missed all of the buildings where all of the people were waiting as if trapped, waiting to die. The aircraft came to rest in the only clear area that could possibly hold such a horrible event. It hit squarely in the vacant field.

The mission planners in the squadron were singed by the ball of flame and showered with glass from the exploding windows, but no one died. The workers in the operations building were pelted with burning debris, but no one died. The shoppers at the BX ran for cover. Their cars and forgotten packages suffered some, but no one died. Even the jogger on the road won his race with death. Its hot breath came so close that his neck was burned but he won. He didn't die.

What precipitated the event can be analyzed but will never be known for sure. For some reason, as the tanker was approaching the field, some range of control was lost. Many hours will be spent in simulators and at roundtable discussions trying to determine what caused the loss. At some point a decision will be made. But no one will ever know for sure what really happened aboard that aircraft. When the smoke cleared and the wreckage was sifted it was found that only one person on the ground met death with the ill-fated crew of the stratotanker. Of all the possible observers who might have died, only one was struck down. And soon it became known that that one was the most unbelievable of all.

The man who died on the ground was the man who should have been on the aircraft that day. It was a young boom operator who was unable to be with them for the flight. It was his fate to die in the crash with his crew. Fate reached out; death reached out, to claim its own.

THE GHOST OF
CHARLIE FIFTY-FOUR

*G*UAM *was like a gift to me. Even in the face of war I felt I had escaped the snows of upstate New York for the white sand beaches and tropical breezes of this island paradise. But I found out that there are worse things than snow. It took quite a while to piece together all the facts of the following story and I'm not sure it's all entirely accurate. You see, I didn't meet Lieutenant Sommers until after his first flight from Guam.*

The island of Guam is the most western part of the United States. An American territory since 1950, it lies on the far side of the international date line. Guamanians are American citizens and, as such, think of Guam as "where America's day begins."

The biggest island of the Marianas chain, Guam is still a

tiny Pacific island. Thirty miles long from north to south, it is only four miles wide at its narrowest point.

Small as it is, during the Vietnam War Guam became host to one of the biggest buildups of aircraft and airmen ever seen. The Pacific headquarters of the Strategic Air Command since 1954, Andersen Air Base on the northeastern tip of the island became one of the biggest bomber bases ever constructed. At the high point of US involvement in the Vietnam War over 150 B-52s, the world's biggest bombers, were stationed at Guam. So much metal was piled on the end of the island, so many aircraft, munitions, and support equipment, that it was a commonly held belief that one more plane would cause the island to tip over into the sea. It was mentioned only partially in jest.

With the advent of "Operation Bullet Shot" in 1972 the activity on Guam intensified. The biggest maintenance force ever assembled at one base worked impossible hours to ensure that the giant aircraft turned and flew constantly. Crews, used to flying two sorties a month, were flying two to three times a week. Weapon loaders were loading more bombs each day than some bases had ever seen. The airfield was a maze of activity barely controlled by a maintenance staff ensconced in a tower at the south end of the field. It was joked that there were more aircraft on Andersen than there were parking spaces. Some bombers had to be taxied constantly, like a New York car looking for an open spot by the curb.

The crews of the giant bombers found life as hurried as the rest of the personnel. Normal stateside operations called for a full day of mission planning, three to four hours of preflight, and at least two days of recovery after the mission. Here incountry, the operation was squeezed into a few hours to prepare and then a rushed entry into the aircraft and a sudden launch in a wave of aircraft. Ironically, crews found that the only place to relax was in the air. Sorties from Guam to Vietnam took over eighteen hours. It was thought of as eighteen hours of boredom broken up by a few minutes of sheer panic.

Into the midst of this chaotic dance was thrust a young man, a first lieutenant named Justin O. Sommers. He was the proverbial wet-behind-the-ears lieutenant, his silver bars as new as his navigator wings.

The normal order of integration for a new navigator in the Strategic Air Command was much more relaxed. The new nav usually finished Combat Crew Training School, where he was introduced to the venerable B-52. He then cleaned up various required units like water and land survival schools, and reported to an operational unit for more training. His first flight at his unit was called a dollar ride and usually involved no more than a ride to watch how a fully trained crew operated. He was then given several flights with his crew to learn his job and, finally, he was evaluated by his friendly neighborhood Standardization Board instructor to see if he could do the job.

For Justin Sommers there was no gentle breaking-in period. He had been hustled through a succession of accelerated courses with all the time to breathe taken out. Instead of leaving Castle Air Force Base at this point for his permanent base, he was shifted down the road to the Replacement Training Unit. The purpose of this unit was to turn the young nav into a steely-eyed killer capable of navigating the D model of the B-52. The D model had been given the "big belly" modification to allow it to carry over a hundred bombs and was fast becoming the workhorse of the Vietnam war.

As soon as RTU had scared him to death, the Air Force shipped Lieutenant Sommers to his base of assignment. He was there for just long enough to set his bags down. He was thrown on the next available cattle car, a charter airliner, headed for Guam.

The air carrier deposited the young man at the base, a taxi took him to the squadron, and the operations officer informed him that he was happy to have him aboard and that he was late already.

Usually, even in times of war, the squadron was able to give a new man, especially one as new as Justin, time to settle in. But the war, and especially Andersen's part of the war, had suddenly intensified. Every man was needed yesterday.

The major apologized but directed Lieutenant Sommers to grab his flying gear and meet a bus in front of the squadron. His dollar ride was going to be a doozy!

The bus took the dazed lieutenant to the flight line. He was amazed by the activity. Everywhere were trucks, buses, cars, bomb wagons. In the midst of it all, B-52s were taxiing, taking off, and landing. He drove past row after row of bombers. They were separated from each other by three-sided boxes made of steel and filled with dirt. They were called revetments and had a very special purpose. The military found out on December 7, 1941, that parking aircraft close together was not a great idea. The Japanese learned, to their delight, that they didn't have to hit every aircraft on the ground. Just hitting one on either end of a line led to a very deadly chain reaction. The explosion of one plane caused the explosion of the next, and that caused the next to go up, and so on right down the line. Revetments were invented to stop the possible chain reaction. At first glance it would seem that the steel-reinforced bunkers were meant to prevent damage.

The actual purpose was not to protect aircraft and crew but to contain the damage to a single aircraft.

The bus drove down the taxiway separating the two long runways. The driver glanced at a sheet of paper and pulled to a stop in front of a B-52 levered into one of the revetments.

"Here you are, L.T., Charlie Fifty-four."

The driver indicated the number on the revetment. The lieutenant stepped off the bus and was immediately accosted by a captain in a flying suit.

"Hi, I'm Chip Barnes. You must be Sommers. You're late. We have to mount up right now and get started. I'll be your instructor. Denney Hodges is the radar and he's got all the mission paperwork with him. Jump on up and I'll throw your gear in. We got to get buttoned up right now."

Justin just gaped wide-eyed at the verbal barrage from the captain. He was barely able to nod at what he thought must be the appropriate places. Before he knew it he was in the nav station ejection seat and strapping in for a flight. His first mission with a real crew was going to be a real honest-to-goodness war mission. No time to learn.

A few minutes later the big bomber lumbered out of the revetment and headed for the runway. On the way out they passed the bus that had brought Justin to his plane. The driver waved out the window, but the bomber proceeded without notice. The driver shrugged and headed for the next pickup.

Well, I tried, thought the driver. *Maybe the kid won't need his helmet this time.*

In the haste to get Justin aboard, a very important piece of his personal safety gear had been forgotten. A crew flight helmet is never referred to as a crash helmet, but every flyer knows what it's there for.

In SAC the worst thing for a navigator is to be behind the airplane. In school they told him, "you've got to stay ahead of the aircraft. You've got to anticipate, plan ahead, always stay one step in front."

Here, now, on a real flight, in a real war, Justin felt like he was so far behind that he was probably still back in the parking stub. He sweated in the cellar of the big, black bomber. Paper flew and pencils broke. He and the senior nav, the radar navigator in the seat next to him, strived to keep the big bomber on course in spite of capricious winds and last-minute changes. Justin wrestled with the time control. Everything had to be controlled to the second or they wouldn't have to worry about enemy gunners. They would run into a friendly who was on time and end up in a monumental aluminum shower.

They were in-country and on the bomb run before Justin had time to breathe. His instructor had given quiet instructions and whispered words of encouragement up to this point. Now he was strapped into his seat as the hostile threats made flying more and more dangerous.

The B-52 is one of the few two-storied airplanes in the Air Force. The pilot, copilot, and electronic warfare officer were on the top story, striving to dodge the antiaircraft fire and flaming SAMs or surface-to-air missiles.

Down below, in a windowless room illuminated only by the orange glow of the radar, the nav team prepared to deliver the bomb load. Justin glanced at the radar nav. The RN was an old head, used to the stress of battle. He was refining his aiming and quietly readying the equipment that would deliver over fifty tons of high explosive on the target. The gunner, in his private cockpit in the tail of the aircraft, was calling out SAMs being launched. His voice did not betray the anxiety he must be feeling.

They reached the initial point. Now all the energy of the crew would be directed to putting the bombs on the target. The RN assumed control of the aircraft. Every move of his tracking handle moved the giant bomber closer to the target. Justin counted down the seconds. "Five, four, three, two, one, hack." The bomb lights flashed, the aircraft jumped slightly and its weight suddenly decreased.

"Two's clean, breaking away," said the copilot over the radio.

The mighty bomber executed a sweeping turn to the left, away from the target and the enemy.

"Watch it, Two. You got a SAM coming up at you." The call from the number three aircraft in the cell alerted the pilot. He racked the control column to the left, increasing the bank at the same time he hit the throttles. The missile streaked toward the escaping aircraft.

Down below, the nav team was thrown about by the tight bank. The RN watched his pointed dividers float into the air. He grabbed at them and leaned way over to follow them as they headed for the floor. Justin turned to watch him try to retrieve his tools.

The SAM didn't hit the aircraft. It missed. But even its miss was terrible. The enemy soldier had guessed at the altitude of the bomber and set a proximity fuse. His guess was nearly perfect. The weapon detonated very close to the nose of the aircraft on the left side of the fuselage.

The RN was leaning over, trying to catch his dividers. The explosion took out his panels where just a few minutes ago he had put in the settings for the bombs. He missed the wave of concussion and the flying pieces of his instruments. He was untouched. Justin wasn't so lucky. He barely had time to see the metal panels flying toward him like lawn mower blades.

The instructor watched in horror from the IN seat. Maybe if Justin had been wearing his helmet, he might have been saved. Maybe it wouldn't have made much difference. The exploding panels ended Justin Sommers' short career as a B-52 navigator. The young warrior was decapitated neatly by the panels he had spent the last year learning to use.

But that's not the end of our story. It's only the beginning.

The war in Vietnam and the war activity on Guam didn't slow down. They intensified. But as the activity reached a fever pitch, another activity intensified also. Its effects were slow to advance but relentless.

A load crew arrived at Charlie Fifty-four in the predawn hours of a Sunday not many days after the ill-fated flight of Justin Sommers.

As the crew prepared the bombs for loading the load chief looked around for the ground crew chief. The young airman should have met them at the plane, but he was nowhere to be found. They finally found him huddled in the corner of the adjacent revetment. He was shivering and holding his arms tightly to his body as if the weather had suddenly taken a turn toward winter. But winter in Guam rarely got below seventy-five degrees and this was the middle of summer.

The load chief was finally able to pry some words of explanation out of the young airman. But what he heard left him more confused than ever.

The airman had been dropped off at the aircraft around midnight to start preflight alone. When he jumped off the bus he noticed a helmet bag near the power cart and had assumed that someone had forgotten it. He picked it up, felt the familiar shape of a helmet inside, and climbed up in the airplane to leave it on board. The inside of the bomber was dark except for the light from outside that shined up the hatch.

The airman was startled to see the shape of a crew member sitting in the navigator's seat. The officer was in shadow but it looked like he was doing some paperwork. He was doing paperwork in almost total darkness. The airman just stood on the hatch steps in confusion, trying to let his eyes adjust to the gloom. The shape turned toward him and reached for the helmet in his hand. As it moved into the dim light from the hatch the airman was horrified to see that the body ended above the shoulders. He could clearly see the lieutenant's bars on the flight suit, but there was no head!

The airman dropped the bag and fled from the aircraft. He had been huddled in the corner of the neighboring revetment for hours.

The airman was carted off to the hospital. He was listed as a case of battle fatigue. The long hours had just gotten the better of him. He rotated back to the States early. The load crew found no helmet bag anywhere around the aircraft. And they certainly found no headless lieutenant.

The next incident at Charlie Fifty-four took place after a flight. The B-52 had landed with a hung weapon in the bomb bay. A load team was called to safely remove the weapon. The crew was just departing the area as the team arrived. The chief sent one of his men to open the big bomb bay doors with the cables in the aft wheel well. As they swung open, he lit his flashlight and ducked under the doors to inspect the bomb.

He walked to the back of the bomb bay and lifted his flash to look at the weapon. His light stopped, though, on an object hanging from the catwalk above the bomb bay. As he moved closer for a better look he realized it was a booted foot. He raised the light to find a leg then a torso in a flight suit. He stood with his mouth open in confusion. Suddenly the figure leaned into the light. The head was missing.

The crew chief dropped his light and ran. He forgot that he was under a bomber. He tripped on an object on the ground. He just had time to see what he had tripped on before his head connected with the bomb bay door. It was a helmet, in a helmet bag.

The unconscious crew chief was taken to the hospital. His injuries were judged minor until he came around and started to babble about the headless lieutenant. The doctors decided to reconsider the seriousness of his injury.

In the meantime the stories about the haunted revetment started to gain ground. After a while the rumored occurrences got to be so numerous that no one wanted to work there. Even air crews were starting to refuse to park there. It came to a head when a load crew pulled up to a bomber with a load of Mark 82 five-hundred-pound bombs to load. As the truck slowed to halt the bomb doors suddenly slammed shut.

The crew didn't even stop the truck. They just returned to the hangar and refused to go near the aircraft until it was moved from Charlie Fifty-four. No other crew could be found who would take the job, either.

It is the position of the Air Force that things such as ghosts and goblins do not exist. They have no basis in fact and are, therefore, not officially recognized. It is also a fact that from that day on, even with the ramp as crowded as it was, the Air Force never again used Charlie Fifty-four as a parking space for a B-52.

After that the stories of the headless lieutenant quieted

down, at least in number. But the revetment continued to cause troubles. Numerous times a helmet bag was noticed sitting in the empty parking space. No one ever went to retrieve it, though. And many supervisors of flying were sent out to turn off the lights in the revetment. No one had turned them on but they were burning brightly. And usually the officer would drive all the way to the back wall, turn off the switch, and then see the lights come on by themselves as he drove away.

Whatever the truth of the matter is, the Air Force still does not believe in ghosts. But it doesn't believe in a revetment called Charlie Fifty-four anymore either.

THE SIMULATED SPIRIT

A simulator is a great place to learn about flying and about the intricacies of modern aircraft. After twenty years of flying on B-52s, I actually learned more about the old "Buff" by teaching in the simulator. But I never in my wildest imaginings dreamed that I'd learn something about the supernatural from this electronic marvel.

Some environments are the exact opposite of what is usually required for a haunting. They are too modern, too sterile, too new, for any self-respecting spirit to call home. Scientific and technical, they appear to be almost ghost-proof.

That is certainly the case with the Weapons System Trainer at Minot Air Force Base. It is a marvelously conceived flight simulator for the training of B-52H crew members. Modern and advanced, it is the total antithesis of anything supernatural.

Many years ago the Air Force learned the value of demonstration in instruction. It's much easier to get a lesson across by showing than by telling. It was a lesson that applied especially to aviation. Showing was the best way to teach fledgling pilots. But it was very costly and often impractical to try to demonstrate everything in an aircraft. There just weren't enough air frames or instructor pilots available.

To save money, and time, they came up with the idea of flight simulators. They could be flown and crashed without too great a cost in machines and lives. The first machines were rudimentary, but as the technology of flight improved the simulators improved accordingly.

The WST was a sterling example of the advances of modern technology. Over two hundred software engineers had labored for years to write the reams of code necessary to give birth to the machine. The tasks of the simulator were so involved that fourteen mainframe computers labored in perfect unison to make it operate. Eleven monster disk drives fed the computer the code that took the place of jet fuel in the aircraft being simulated. More than two gigabytes of available memory were necessary to make the imitation of flight seem real. Designers had pored over maps and charts and satellite photos, reducing mountains and fields and streams and forests to ones and zeros arranged in particular computer language. When fed to the computers these ones and zeros were translated into a remarkably accurate picture of the land that the simulator flew over.

Every system of the gigantic bomber was duplicated in the simulator. It had to be accurate; it had to feel right.

Perched on six hydraulically driven legs, the flight station

looked like a cross between a robot and a huge metal spider.
The legs were articulated to allow for every twist and turn
that the aircraft would make as it winged its way through the
simulated sky. Immense pressure lines fed hydraulic blood to
the beast. Computer-driven actuators snapped the station left
and right, up and down in a frenzied mating dance that
looked uncoordinated and strange to the outside observer.

But step inside the flight station and you have stepped
onto the flight deck of the Boeing B-52H Super Stratofortress. All those computers and all those disks and all that
hydraulic fluid and all that power combine to make the illu-
sion real. Sit in the ejection seat confronted by the rows and
rows of glowing, moving, accurate dials and gauges. Look at
the switches and knobs that you know must control the craft.
Strap into the pilot's position and run the multiple throttle
levers slightly forward to give more fuel to the eight powerful engines and hear them roar their hunger. The huge metal
boxes that rested so awkwardly on the forehead of the mechanical arachnid now provide a panoramic view out the
cockpit windows of the earth rushing by hundreds of feet
below the racing bomber. Move the column to the side and
feel the airplane bank and your world tilt into the turn. The
mirage is truly miraculous.

The building that houses the WST is as complete and
modern as the facility it was built to house. The bay where
the flight station weaves and lurches and finally squats at rest
on its silver legs is pristine. The walls shine with fresh earth
tone paint and glow in the shadow-killing glare of halogen
arc lights set into the three-story-high ceiling. Even the
floors shine in their cleanliness. The miles of cable are hidden in tastefully appointed under-floor cable runs or wrapped

neatly in bundles that attach like an umbilical cord to the belly of the monster.

The control facility, full of computer keyboards, oversize glowing display terminals, and silently professional technicians, is as subdued as the flight station bay is bright. It looks like the launching room of a space facility.

Even the offices of the technicians behind the control room are antiseptic and color coordinated.

The technicians who service this modern marvel expect things to go as planned. That doesn't mean that everything will work all the time. They expect things to weaken, circuits to short, diodes to die, chips to flare, and binary coupling to come uncoupled. And they expect this to take place according to the mean-time-between-failure charts and graphs generated by other computers that understand these computers. They expect to be able to fix these failures with the parts ordered and maintained by still other computers.

Late in the night, when the last bomb run has been completed and the last missile has been launched and the last fighter has been avoided; when the last emergency has been solved and the last landing accomplished in spite of grievous battle damage and the last crew member has gone home, the technicians run their diagnostic programs and hunt for the expected problems. All the intelligence and scientific thought that went into this machine gives them the right to expect these things.

What they didn't expect to find was a ghost in the machine. But that is what happened.

It started slowly and was not recognized for what it was for some time.

The earliest occurrence took place after midnight in the console operations room. The room, and in fact the whole building, is entirely divorced from the outside. The total absence of windows prevents the occupants from determining the time or type of day. The carefully controlled temperature and humidity prevent any hint of what mother nature is brewing up outside. The hum of the machines is at first the most insistent sound and then, after acclimatization, an unnoticed background of white noise.

Donaley, the mid-shift supervisor of the technician team, was seated in front of the console screen in a computer-induced trance. His eyes followed the random-appearing dance of alphanumerics across the screen. He was concentrating on the pattern, looking for the single bit that was not in step with the rest. The technician on the other side of the console squatted behind the open doors to the insides of the machine. He had been pulling and reseating the many computer boards to attempt to isolate the one that was causing the problem. He was totally hidden from Donaley's view.

Donaley's concentration was interrupted by the bang of first one then the next equipment door slamming shut.

"What's the matter? You giving up?" He didn't look up from the screen as he asked the question. The only answer he got was the third and final cabinet door slamming shut.

"Did you pull all the boards?" asked Donaley. He rolled his chair back from the console and stretched. He had been locked into an uncomfortable position by his concentration. There was no answer from behind the console.

"Hey, Ted, I asked if you pulled all the boards." This time he raised his voice to be sure his counterpart heard him clearly. Still there was no reply.

"Ted, what the hell's the matter with you?"

"I don't know. What the hell's the matter with you?"

Donaley swung around violently in his chair. The voice

came not from behind the console but from the door to the control room. Ted had apparently exited the room sometime earlier while Donaley was immersed in his inspection of the computer screen.

Ted laughed at his boss's stare and swung around the end of the console.

"Hey, who closed all the cabinet doors?"

Good question, thought Donaley. He was too shaken to speak.

On another night not too long after the first, Donaley was seated at the same console, this time wearing a communications headset. Another technician had drawn the midnight shift and was ensconced in the flight station going through the radio circuits to try and track down a reported problem.

"Pilot, radio one check."

"Rog, one checks."

"Pilot, radio two check."

"Rog, two checks."

"Pilot, HF check."

"Rog, HF checks."

The litany was monotonous and boring, but necessary. Donaley was in the midst of what must have been the nine millionth check when he was interrupted by a light tap on his shoulder.

"Just a minute," he waved the interruption off. "Let me finish this last check."

He heard a cross between a mutter and a whisper from behind his left shoulder but he couldn't make out the words. Removing his headset, he swung around to face the person. There was no one in the room.

Of course there was no one there. Donaley suddenly remembered that he and the technician were the only ones in the locked building that night.

Donaley felt the hairs on the back of his neck stand up as he tried to think who had touched him and whispered in his ear.

Stories about the ghostly visitors started to circulate among the technicians. They found that several had had unexplained things happen to them individually. Most had been afraid to say anything. To paraphrase the poet, it's better to say nothing and appear to be a fool than to open your mouth and remove all doubt.

But now that the shift super had let them know about his brushes with the supernatural, other happenings started to be told.

A tech related his experience on the graveyard shift while he was working alone in the console room. The doors to the study and briefing rooms are held open by electromagnets as a fire safety precaution. If a fire breaks out, the power is removed from the building and the doors shut automatically to prevent the spread of fire. As he worked alone on the computer, suddenly one by one the doors to the rooms slammed shut. If power had been lost from the building, the doors should have shut all at once. But the power stayed on. He watched in shock as each door slammed in turn, right down the row. He then left the console room for a more brightly lit and heavily populated maintenance room.

A stranger happening took place in the flight station itself. Dennis, one of the day technicians, was helping out the night crew with a persistent motion problem. He was "flying" the station while the other two techs monitored his progress at the console.

When the box is under motion, its occupants are totally

isolated from the room. To enter the station, you must cross a drawbridge that raises away when the motion system is activated. The station then lifts up on its legs to prepare to simulate the flight. The occupants are now suspended twelve feet above the floor. Anyone on the outside of the station would prevent the station's rise. The catwalk is covered with a pressure sensitive flooring that inhibits motion, and lights a warning light at the console to show when anyone steps on the station or even touches it. So Dennis was completely isolated from others as he flew the plane above the computer earth.

The gentle rocking motion of the simulator and the background noise of the jets worked in unison to lull him. He was almost dozing when suddenly a hand slapped the back of his head. It was the kind of slap a pilot would use to jump-start his copilot's brain when he botched something.

It definitely got Dennis's brain working. He punched the emergency stop, shutting off the power to the system, ripped off his seat belt, and bolted for the door. He almost pitched over the railing. The drawbridge had not yet dropped in place. He was on it and running for the steps before the pumps had released all the pressure. His faith in modern machines was somewhat shaken. But the best was yet to come.

Friday night is the only night that the trainer is completely shut down. The process of turning it off is involved and must be followed exactly to prevent damage to the components.

Ted and Ron were working in the flight station as Jerry worked outside the building to clean up the area. Ted was shutting down the pilot's side as Ron did the same with the copilot's side. The windows were blank. They had already turned off the computer that produced the visuals. Suddenly the window blossomed with a picture of the runway at Minot.

"Wonder why Jerry turned on the visuals?" asked Ted. "You finish up here and I'll go see what's happening."

He left to check on the computer room. He was surprised to find the visual computer working away but the room totally empty of human beings. He tracked Jerry down in the maintenance shed, where he was laboring to store a garden tractor. Jerry followed him back to the bay to see what was going on.

Ron was standing on the catwalk of the flight station as they entered the bay. He just shrugged his shoulders when they told him they didn't know how the visuals came back on.

"You two go ahead and pull the plug on the computers and I'll police up the console room," he said.

They went into the supercooled computer room and started the process that removed all power from the banked computers. As the thinking machine slowly ground down, the silence became overwhelming. When the last switch had been thrown, they reentered the bay.

Above them, on the catwalk, Ron was standing in the door to the flight station. He appeared to be frozen to the spot.

"I thought you guys were going to turn everything off?" He yelled the question to the men below without turning from his perusal of the flight station.

"What d'ya mean? We did," answered Ted. "It's dead as a doornail."

"Dead, huh?" Ron turned from the doorway. His face was white and his eyes were wide.

"Maybe you better come up here and take a look at this then."

The two technicians bolted up the stairs and into the flight station. There they stared at a technological impossibility. For the flight station was anything but dead. Without the benefit of software or computers or even electrical power the station was up and ready to go. All the lights blazed, all the gauges registered, all the dials moved. The sound of eight powerful simulated engines poured from the speakers. The windows glowed with the scene of the runway stretched out in front of the plane, clear and ready for the next flight.

But who was going to make that flight?

The three men locked and left the building. According to the laws of electricity as they knew them, the simulator was completely shut down. If someone or something was running the computers with different laws, they were content to let them have at it.

Much conjecture has been expended concerning the ghost of the simulator. A ghost is usually tied to a place from his past or a place where he died. But the sim is completely new and modern. It was built of new and sterile parts. The building was constructed for the sole purpose of housing the simulator. Even the ground that it sits on has no history that would attract a spirit. As far back as can be determined, the land was vacant, first as prairie, then as farmland, and finally as a vacant lot on an Air Force base.

There is only one part of the simulator that was not constructed originally for its use, and therein may lie the answer. While the flight station looks like an airplane on the inside, the outside only needs to look like a box. And for the most part it does. But the designer was given the opportunity to add some flare to the device. Old models of the B-52 were retired and, after years of faithful service, were on their way to the smelter to be recycled into newer vehicles. He was

able to rescue at least part of one of the old Buffs (Big Ugly
Fat Fellows) and incorporate it into the modern simulator.
The skin covering the cockpit and windows was removed
and included on the flight station nose.

Maybe this piece of the old war bird held more than metal
and glass and plastic and rubber. Maybe it was the home of
something long dormant and resting. Maybe the simulation
aroused it, attracted it, and now amuses it.

Or maybe another type of Air Force just needs the practice.

WHITE CHIEF

*A*S a young man sitting nuclear alert, I never really felt the enormity of my situation until one incident brought it all into perspective. We were on alert at a West Coast base when a computer in the early warning system made a mistake. As a result of the glitch we almost launched the fleet. After that I knew the meaning of real fear. Sometimes the known is worse than the unknown.

What's the scariest place you can think of? Think it's an old, ramshackle *Psycho*-like mansion with an infamous past and an unsavory present? The kind that you joke about with your friends at school, scaring and daring and parading your courage? But your bragging freezes in your imagination as you pass the house on the far side of the street. You know that the undoubtedly haunted hovel will star in your dreams. Is that your idea of frightening?

Maybe you grew up on splatter flicks and movie special effects creatures. No scary old house for your nightmares. You need alien claws and technoshock surroundscare to get your teeth chattering. Only Freddy's smile can call up your chills.

Let me tell you of a scarier place. A place that demands your attention and can steal your breath and your heartbeat in a fraction of a whimper. How about living and working in the exact center of a bull's-eye? It's not visible and it's not always the same size but it's always there and it's very real. One more thing. It's got the most powerful, deadly, devastating weapon ever dreamed of aimed right at its heart.

This place is an Air Force base in the heart of the heartland. That means it's in a place that's not very populated and definitely not a must-see on the jet set tour.

Grand Forks Air Force Base is located near the Red River Valley of that great and frozen state of North Dakota. The "Forks" is not a major base as military bases go, but it has major standing in another league. It's a senior stalwart in the coldest of battles. It is armed with weapons of Armageddon proportion. Its nuclear arsenal is formidable. An astute observer noticed that North Dakota, given sovereign status, would become the third largest nuclear power in the world.

Generations of warriors assigned to this base went about their careers and their lives in the middle of this bull's-eye. The enemy knew of them and their power. They were required by command and by law to feign ignorance of their own power to the public. "I can neither confirm nor deny that," was the only statement they could make. But they knew the weapons were there. And their enemy knew that the weapons were there. And they knew the enemy had trained his own doomsday device at them. So they lived and worked and played and slept in the bull's-eye, never certain of anything except their duty.

The fear was there. It was a constant undercurrent that seasoned their lives. And it wasn't just the fear of what their enemy would do if given the chance. It was also the fear of what they could do to themselves if they weren't very careful and very good.

They knew they were living on time not borrowed but wrested from a cruel fate. Years before, when the weapons were new and the threat was new and computers were new and filled whole buildings, a private company was asked to look at the fledgling nuclear force. The brass were concerned about the growing number of accidents involving nuclear weapons.

They went outside their carefully groomed force to a company famed for objectivity and analytical skill. They asked them to study, delve, question, and observe. And they asked them to ask their big-as-a-house computing machine two questions.

The first was, "Will we have an accident resulting in a nuclear detonation?" And the second was only to be asked if the first resulted in a yes. It was, simply, "When?"

The company dug and worked and gathered and finally fed all their careful study to the computer. And they asked the first question. Without hesitation the electronic oracle said, "Yes."

The company personnel who fed data into the new thinking machine suddenly lost some of their celebrated objectivity. The machine that they served and to some degree worshiped, had just predicted death on a monumental scale.

Fearfully, then, they prepared the second question. The tubes glowed and the wires vibrated as the metal mind contemplated the question. Then it unfurled a strip of paper from an orifice.

The scientists took the answer from their creation. Afraid to look yet afraid of not knowing, they unraveled the answer. As if in jest, the machine had named a range of dates for the catastrophe. But the dates were for five years in the past. It took a moment for the implication to soak in. The computer was telling them that they were living on borrowed time. The event could take place at almost any moment unless something changed to avert it.

This information was rushed to the military officials who had ordered the study. For the first time in peacetime the military command did not hesitate. They called in all the safety and security experts they could find and began the task of redesigning the control of these weapons of mass destruction.

The basic rules they formulated for the protection of these most-destructive of weapons have survived for over thirty years. It is a credit to the rules that the country that houses the weapons has survived also.

Those rules continue to guide the guardians of atomic weapons. The Strategic Air Command, the central figure of the nuclear triad, is the guardian of most of the nuclear weapons on American soil.

If you have ever been on a SAC base, you will know that they take their control of these weapons seriously.

At a base like Grand Forks, the reminders start when you cross the boundary of the base. Or when you attempt to cross the boundary. No one gets on the base without the express consent of the base commander. That consent comes in the form of documents, orders and such. Everything must be in order.

After you enter the base, security doesn't let up. In fact it gets tighter the nearer you get to the weapons. A Strategic Air Command base has two distinct police forces. There's the normal type that you would expect in any community. The law enforcement group handles the routine police business of the base. They patrol the streets, handing out moving violations and parking tickets where needed. They protect the businesses on base and make sure that everything runs smoothly and legally.

But there's another police force that few know of. Its job is to guard the weapons of mass destruction. Its members apply the rules that came from that early study. They enforce those rules strictly. They know that everyone is living on borrowed time. The job must be done right or the sword of Damocles will fall as predicted. They are dead serious about their work.

As you get closer to the areas where the weapons rest, the control becomes ominous. You see the tall fences, not one but rows of them. The area in between is sterile and swept. If you knew a little about the job, you would be chilled to learn that these well-maintained spaces between the fences are called killing zones.

Look closer at the fences. They are topped not by normal barbed wire but by something unique. It looks like the concertina wire used in Vietnam but it's different. It's flat and sharpened. It's called razor wire by the troops and is so deadly that we are restricted by wartime conventions from using it on foreign soil.

Move a little closer and you start to see the signs. If you can get close enough to read one, you will see phrases like "no unauthorized entry," and "express written permission of the command authority," and "use of deadly force is authorized."

But if you can get close enough to read the signs, it has already been determined that you have a legitimate reason to be there. The security guards have methods of surveillance that even the people who work there have no knowledge of. They are dead serious in their work.

Within the alert area, where the bombers sit poised and loaded for the final war, the security is intense. Even the crew members who work there daily must prove their right and need to be there a hundred times a day. No one strolls idly around the bombers. You must have a purpose to be there.

Each aircraft has its own personal guard. No one gets within fifty feet of the bomber without proper authorization and recognition. And there are guards who watch the guards. And another echelon behind that one to watch the watchers. Trust is not a given here.

On a dark fall night, the guard on alert sortie number three walked his post by the giant bomber. The aircraft was lit by stadium lights high above the ramp, but the structure of the huge bomber blocked the light in many areas. The aircraft was wreathed in shadows.

The airman paced the line around the bomber, constantly alert, his eyes sweeping the darkness. It might seem to be a dull job. But SAC did a lot to prevent boredom from being a player in nuclear security.

The young man knew that his movements were constantly being watched and evaluated. Many agencies were given the job of testing the security he provided. Any of those could suddenly attempt to penetrate his area to gauge his ability.

Punishment for failing to pass these tests was immediate and painful. Any member of this elite force who failed could find himself the exact opposite of his profession: a prisoner.

Sweeping his area of control, the security policeman paced the line. Suddenly, his eyes registered movement from the periphery of a large shadow. He rushed to the point of the aircraft boundary, charging his weapon as he ran. Even if it was a test, he must react as if it were the real thing. The evaluators would identify themselves before he could use any of that deadly force.

But it wasn't a test. High above the alert area, in a darkened control tower, the next echelon of security scanned banked monitors of television screens. The low-light cameras covered every square inch of the compound. Just to make sure that the cameras missed nothing, a guard paced the catwalk outside the tower, watching everything through high-powered binoculars.

Suddenly the attention of these overseers was riveted to the area of sortie number three. The muffled popping coming from that area wouldn't have meant much to an untrained observer. Certainly not the end of the world. But that's how the guardians above the aircraft took it.

Immediately, sirens rang out. Both men were on their radios alerting all agencies and all security police on the base. Calls went out to a different part of the airfield. A helicopter, on twenty-four-hour alert, started its engine with a bang and a whine. The pilot pulled it off the ground and swung violently toward the alert facility as the last armed soldier clambered aboard.

All over the base, high-ranking officers were running for their vehicles. With red lights flashing, they converged on the heart of the base.

Everyone was responding to the same message. Everyone was reacting to the same rush of adrenaline that accompanied the words.

"Shots fired! Shots fired in the alert facility!"

It is safe to say that an army was converging on that contested part of the Air Force base. And they converged with grim determination. For a prime directive was that atomic weapons would not be damaged, destroyed, or removed from the control of the Air Force, regardless of the cost.

There would be no exceptions.

The advance arm of the protectors approached the line around alert sortie three very cautiously. Attempts had been made to reach the guard responsible for that zone. There had been no response to repeated radio calls.

The senior noncom, a Vietnam veteran, signaled to the forces arrayed behind him to stay put. He crawled forward to the side of the bomber opposite from where the shots had come. Looking under the nose of the silent bomber, he could see the form of the guard lying on the ground. He could tell that the young man was in a defensive posture, with his weapon pointed into the shadows behind the bomber.

"Hey, kid, this is Sergeant Stander. What have you got out there?" The sergeant's words were delivered in a calm, soothing tone. He didn't want to startle the heavily armed and obviously frightened airman.

"I . . . I don't know. I don't know what I got, Sarge," came the shaky reply. "It's out there, though. I know it's out there."

"Permission to approach your post?" said the sergeant. Formality was required in security situations.

"Permission granted," came back to him from the young cop. "But be careful. He's still out there."

The NCO whispered into his radio, then crawled the short distance to the prone airman.

Before he could ask, the airman blurted out his observations.

"He was right over there. Behind the tail of number four. He was on a horse, a big one, a white one. He looked real white, too. Just riding up there on the edge of the pad like this was some damned circus show. All those feathers in his hat, he looked like something out of a history book. I yelled at him and I know he heard me cause he looked right at me. But he didn't halt. He just kept riding behind the other airplane. I think I got him. I let him have it with about ten rounds. I must have hit him."

The sergeant was listening to this recitation with ever-growing disbelief on his face. He finally interrupted the litany with a question of his own.

"You mean to tell me that you were shooting at an Indian? A big white Indian with feathers, on a big white horse?"

"Yeah, yeah, I know it sounds weird, but that's what it was."

The airman was intent on surveying the dark for the return of his nemesis. He didn't see the sergeant slip his handgun from its holster. He pointed the barrel at the head of the young man. He would give him one chance to surrender his weapon. But then, no nuclear weapon can ever be endangered, whatever the cost. And the young security policeman had just become expendable.

"Just move your hands away from your weapon, real slowly," the sergeant started, when suddenly he saw movement in the darkness.

The horse glided silently from behind the neighboring bomber. It glowed with a reflected light that came from no earthly source. Its rider glowed palely from the same source. The tall Indian turned slowly to regard the two men lying on the concrete. He watched them for a long moment, but no expression crossed his face. Then he raised one hand in a gesture of recognition usually reserved for fellow warriors. The horse moved forward of its own volition and the pair faded from view.

Officially the incident was classified as an accidental discharge of an automatic weapon. Many of the young policeman's peers were curious about the circumstances of the incident. Weapons had been known to discharge accidentally before, but the airman in charge had always been severely punished for the accident. This airman was not even reprimanded. His story of the events of the evening was never formally put into writing. But informally the story made the rounds. What made the fantastic story even more fantastic was the senior sergeant's refusal to say anything about the night in question.

Only one other time did the events of that night replay themselves in somewhat like fashion. A bomber crew was leading a three-ship group of bombers out of the parking area for a night launch. As they taxied down the dark strip of concrete to the runway, they came abreast of the Alert facility.

Suddenly the lead ship came to a halt in the middle of the taxiway. The crews in the planes behind the stalled bomber made repeated calls to their lead ship, but they received no answer.

Finally the supervisor of flying called lead to ask what was the problem.

"A . . . SOF . . . we've got a malfunctioning gauge here. Would you send out maintenance?"

After the mission was flown the crew was questioned

about the so-called malfunction. No problem had been found when the maintenance personnel arrived. And the mission flew without a hitch. The entire crew testified that the gauge had been malfunctioning. That was a little strange in itself, because only the pilot and copilot should have been able to see the gauge from their crew positions. No one thought to ask what the whole crew had been doing in the front of the cockpit.

And, when questioned unofficially by other crew members, the crew remained adamant about the events of that night. They saw the gauge. It wasn't working. That was the only reason they stopped. They didn't stop for some guy on a horse. Some guy who looked like an Indian chief. Some guy who was all white. Some guy who vanished while they were all watching him. Nope, that's not the way it happened. Just ask the aircraft commander. We only stopped because the gauge was broken.

Before the bomber taxied at Grand Forks, and before the bombs were built, and before the base was even built, this part of North Dakota was a desolate place. It was not even well loved by the Indians who had to live there. In fact one tribe referred to it as "the place that's not any good to walk across."

Why then would the spirit of an ancient warrior choose this particular spot to haunt?

Maybe there's another line of protection for the terrible weapons at Grand Forks. A last line.

THE WELCOMING COMMITTEE

*T*HE *best thing about a military life is probably the traveling. It's strange that it is also the worst thing about military life. Being uprooted on a regular basis leaves scars on the soul. Finally there comes a time when you say enough. I will live here and move no more. That decision comes to all of us eventually. Usually it comes before it's too late. Usually—but not always.*

Over the hill and around the bend, the headlights pick out the start of the town—the new town. The buildings are bathed in bleak moonlight. They look faded, strange, wrong somehow. All of the requirements are met. Everything that is necessary to make a town is there, and yet. It's wrong, all wrong. The gas station sells the kind of gas you buy but it's laid out wrong. It's on the wrong side of the street. The grocery store you just passed looks adequate but different, forbidding maybe. You'll never get used to shopping there. Not after the pleasant store you left behind in the other town.

Here and there, in spite of the late hour, you see people. People walking, people driving. All strange, all wrong. Ax murderers and deviants all of them.

The town thins and then is gone and you're left with the road and just a sign that says, "Airbase" and points rudely ahead. In your mind you sigh and then start when you hear it echoed aloud.

It's too late for your daughter to be up, but there she is at the rear window of the car. She clutches her Boobear and watches the town, new town, recede in the distance. You know that what she's really seeing is the old town, the old home, the old friends, now left behind. This new town is a poor imitation of home, strange and frightening.

Finally the journey is over. Here's the main gate to the new base. You wanted the long trip to end a couple of days ago and now that it has, you're not so sure. It means the comfortable old base that you knew so well is relegated to the status of memory. You just killed it by driving onto the new base, your base now. Have to call the old home "Base X" from now on. Just a bunch of memories of a place that has no real texture any more.

Directions. Turn here, right there, through this light, past this stop sign. Nighttime makes it even more of a maze. All purposeless direction and no sense. Is this right or should I have turned there? Each landmark is just a thing, not yet THE bank or THE store or THE gym, but just a bunch of places. It's so lonely pulling up, tearing roots loose, going, leaving, moving.

This is it. Look, they call it a hotel. Is that quaint or is it pretentious? Must be the latter but have to be fair. Everything seems pretentiously inept when you're not a part of it. Nothing to feel proud of because nothing belongs to you, yet.

Your weary bunch piles out of the car, still vibrating to the rhythm of the road. Muscles tingle and creak as you enter the office.

Everyone stands huddled in a pool of light, the only warm spot in the strangeness of this room. The clerk reluctantly notices your group and tears himself away from the quiet television.

"Name?" he greets you.

"Ah . . . Simms . . . Joe Simms . . . Sergeant Simms, with two m's."

"Orders?"

"Yeah, here. We just got here from . . ."

"Reservation?"

"What?"

"Do you have a reservation?"

"Oh, yes, yes, our sponsor made it for us."

"I'll check."

Rude, but have to give him the benefit of the doubt. Probably a pretty boring job. After all, he's just a clerk, not a welcoming committee.

"Sign here and here. The TLQ is at the end of Fourth. Take this street two blocks, left at the stop sign, then right at the light. Building 208. No pets. One week maximum. Clean towels over there on the table."

You collect your towels and head for the door, trying to remember the directions.

"Welcome to Griffiss Air Force Base."

Everyone turns to say thanks for a pleasant word finally, only to see that he's gone back to the television. Gotcha. A sarcastic greeting is worse than none at all. Always someone who can't stand a place. You hope for the best. This will be a good assignment, just as good as the last one; maybe even better.

Building 208 is there but it doesn't seem to be at the end of the directions. Must have misunderstood. You found it anyway so, no sweat.

The parking lot is full of strange cars with a profusion of different plates in a wide variety of colors. They look like pushcarts from old pictures of immigrants, stuffed full of the junk that is necessary to start a new life. They are soiled with the mud of many roads all converging on this strange new place.

At the door, there's an envelope tacked by the bell. You open it after you put your little one in the single bed by the window, already asleep. She stayed up long enough to confirm her certainty that this would be a bad place. She sleeps fitfully, dreaming of the home that's now someone else's home and the friends that are just letters and pictures.

The envelope unfolds a ray of sunlight in this dismal process called moving. It's from your sponsor and it's a genuine welcome from someone who went out of his way to understand.

It ends on a happy note.

"You guys are really in luck. Went by the housing office yesterday to check on your position on the wish list. Guess what. They have a house for you to look at already. Somebody canceled out or passed on it or something and you got moved up. Usually takes a couple of months to snag a place here. The town doesn't have much in the way of rentals. Must be an omen. You guys are going to love it here.

Give me a call tomorrow morning after you get a good rest. I'll take you over to see the place."

Moves in the military are a way of life. They are accepted and expected. And in spite of this forewarning they are still one of the most painful things about being a soldier. To be sure, Uncle Sugar pays for everything when he moves you. But you always come up short. You always lose. You lose friends, you lose places, and you lose a sense of belonging that takes longer to get back each time.

The military takes some of the trouble out of moving by providing you help along the way and a home when you get to your new base.

Base housing is a good deal but, contrary to civilian belief, it's not free. You lose your housing allowance, a lump sum from your salary that may make the house a good deal or a bad deal depending on off-base housing prices at your new location. And you're always reminded that the house belongs to the government. You are only borrowing it for a while. And you better take real good care of the government's building.

The morning sun burns away the shadows and some of the strangeness goes with it. You meet your sponsor, a nice guy who was in the same boat as you a couple of months ago. He can still remember and understand the disorientation caused by moving. He goes out of his way to show you around and point out the nice things about the new base.

It's all still too new to be home. Everything still suffers by comparison but some of that is starting to fade. When you get to the house your good fortune goes a long way toward setting things to rights.

The house is beautiful even if it is Air Force. It's more than you expected. Usually the houses on a base tend to be duplexes, and triplexes and even quadruplexes, all the same and all pushed together. You have lived in the worst and always seemed to be able to make the best of it. Neighbors help, probably because of shared adversity.

But now, here is a separate, one-family building that looks amazingly like a normal house. How did you get so lucky? How indeed?

In the days that followed, you and your family stay busy with the thousands of things that need to be done to get a new household started. The moving company is called to deliver the furniture. The furniture that fit so well in the last home refuses to go into this one. Everything must be moved around and changed and experimented with until the angle looks just right, or at least all right for now.

You have to get used to work. Your family has work to do also. They have to find the grocery store and the best way to get to the Exchange. They have to track down stores and schools and banks and telephone offices and gas stations. But during all the running around and searching and hunting, the process of turning this house into a home is taking place.

After the second week the house is starting to become your home. A neighbor stops by to welcome you and your wife.

"See by your license that you were stationed at Base X. We were too. Seems like a thousand years ago. This place is just as good. Better, in some ways."

Then, in what seems like a more cautious tone, "How do you like the house?" It doesn't seem to be just a polite question. She is very interested in the answer.

Your wife, somewhat bewildered by the way the question

is asked, nevertheless can't help but exclaim about the wonderful house and your good fortune in getting it.

"Yeah, well, I hope you stay longer than the last bunch. They decided real sudden to move downtown."

"Why? Is there something wrong with this house?" She is curious about the attitude of her new neighbor.

"No, no, nothing wrong. Nothing that I know of. Wish we had a single."

There is something a little too emphatic in the neighbor's denial but your wife decides to let it pass.

In the days and nights to come she thinks back to this conversation.

Things start slowly. It seems that the shock of moving has infected every member of the Simms family with a case of forgetfulness. Everyone starts to lose things. Nothing big, just irritating. If Mrs. Simms is sure the car keys are on the desk, they aren't found until she looks on the bedroom dresser. And if you are sure that you left the checkbook in your coat, it turns up in the kitchen cabinet. Even your little girl, Sherry, complains that her dolls are playing hide-and-seek when she wants to play school.

It doesn't seem anything but annoying until things start to turn up in the most unlikely places. What had prompted you to leave your ring in the flour canister? And why did Mrs. Simms ever put her silver napkin holder out in the garage in the lawn mower basket? It is as if some little imp is pressing the limits of possibility to see how far he can go before someone gets suspicious.

When your wife finds the dog staring stupidly at the doll's head in his food dish, things finally get to be too much. She can't wait to tell her husband about the rash of lost-and-founds.

That night, after listening to your wife recite a list of improbabilities, you consider the strange occurrences as you drive down to the base minimart. You recognize a neighbor in the line with you. He introduces himself.

"Oh, you must be the one who moved into that strange house on the corner."

You register surprise at this description of your new house.

"Why do you call it strange?"

"No reason really. It just seems to be empty more than it's occupied. And there must be something wrong with the electricity because the lights keep going on and off even when nobody's living there. You notice anything strange?"

You consider the question. You decide that the rash of missing items doesn't really qualify as strange.

"Nope. Nothing out of the ordinary. It's a real nice house."

"You're probably right. What do I know? Nice to meet you anyway."

During the next couple of days you think more and more about your "strange" house. You finally stop by the housing office to see if you can find out anything about it.

When the clerk comes to the window, you suddenly think this whole thing is pretty dumb. What are you doing here? The clerk recognizes you from the day the house was assigned.

"What can I do for you, Sergeant Simms?"

"Ah . . . I just wondered. Is there anything unusual about that house you gave me?" you finally manage to stammer. Your question sounds foolish even before you finish asking it.

"Is there something wrong with the house?" The woman seems almost defensive.

"No, well, no nothing really."

"Do you want to lodge a complaint about the house?"

"No, no complaint." You're really confused by her attitude.

"Then I guess we can be of no further help to you, Sergeant Simms. Good day."

You say good day to her as she is already turning away and leave more disturbed than when you came in.

A few days later the house finally becomes a comfortable place to relax in and sleep in. You hope it will just keep getting more homey.

Mrs. Simms wakes, confused. It's only 3:00 A.M. but something disturbs her. "What is it?" she thinks. "Oh, the baby. The baby is crying." Not too loudly but mothers have well-tuned hearing.

"Whose turn is it for the night patrol?" She still laughs at her husband's term for the late-night baby comforting chores.

Confusion. That joke is at least three years old. It came from back when they had a baby. Sherry is a grown-up five-year-old who has no residual baby in her. She has been sleeping through the night for years now.

Must be the neighbors' child. These triplexes might save the government money but they sure don't make for quiet nights. She tries to avoid it but she learns more than she wants to about her neighbors though the walls. Must be Jenney's girl. She had hard times with every little illness that infants were prone to.

Memory intrudes. Jenney was one of the committee who fared her well. Mrs. Simms doesn't live in the triplex with Jenney and her baby anymore. She doesn't live in a triplex anymore. That can't be a baby in the house or the building. The Simms family is the only family in this house.

She stiffens and grabs her husband's hand reflexively.

"I know," you answer her unasked question. "I hear it too."

"Who is it? What is it?"

You listen together as the baby cries. Sad and lonely sound. So helpless. So lost.

It's as if you've turned a corner or opened another door in the house. Suddenly everyone is treated to all manner of strange sounds.

At night there are footsteps. Slow, pacing steps always ending in the unused bedroom between your room and Sherry's. Cupboards open and close as if someone is looking for something. Looking but not too intent on finding. Just searching for something to do. Suddenly the beautiful house that had started becoming a home is just a building again. You try to overlook and disregard the unusual but it's impossible. Sleep becomes a commodity in short supply for all. Tempers flare and cool and flare again much too often.

A feeling of sadness begins to pervade. But it seems to be a borrowed sadness. Nothing in your lives would account for the degree or flavor of sadness you feel.

Late one night in April, two months after you moved in and one month after you found the house owned by another entity, the two of you lie in the darkness. There are no sounds except those of the living. In a way that is worse. You wait. And you wonder. What next?

You wake surprised that you dozed off. There's your wife, standing at the window in the dark. You watch her without speaking. Even turned from you you can see the sadness in her. You long to take it away, to start over. This has not been a good move.

As if sensing your empathy, she turns slowly from the window. You see that she is sad, very sad indeed, but she is not your wife.

You wait again at the same desk in the housing office, but this time you know why you are here.

"I'm sorry, but I have to ask," you explain to the same clerk. "I need another house. If I can get one on base, great. But I have to move my family. I can't explain it, but I have to get out of that house."

"No need to explain, Sergeant." She sighs as if this is something she expected. "Just sign here and we'll get you in a new place tomorrow. Won't be a single; probably have to be a quad, but that's the best we can do."

"No, no, a quad'll be fine."

You sign the document quickly, then turn to leave. You hesitate.

"What is it? What's wrong with that house?"

"I don't know that anything is officially wrong with that dwelling." She looks hard into your eyes.

"If you have some time, take a look at some old newspapers at the library. Especially the one for the fourteenth of February, ten years ago."

Later that afternoon, you sit back from the microfilm viewer. You think what it must have been like. To be a young mother, a thousand miles from home, on a strange base, when the letter arrived in the hand of the base chaplain. When the words finally found meaning that night, that her husband really wouldn't be coming back, back to the same house that you live in now.

They found her in the baby's bedroom by the tiny form of her child. Both were still and composed. Both were cold. The paper had printed her picture, from her wedding. The expression was worlds apart, but it was the same girl that had looked out of your window.

We always lose something when we move. But sometimes we find something. Something that someone else left behind. Or someone.

DEADSTICK LANDING

*W*AR *is the strangest way of life. At first you are petrified with fright. So many ways to die. So many chances to take. But then you live through a few of them and realize it's not so bad. And then you start to lose friends to stupid mistakes and fatal illnesses that have nothing to do with war. And then it becomes really frightening: all these new ways to die and all the old ones, too. And then out of nowhere you become convinced that there is something else beyond all this death. Strange things happen in war.*

When Harry Lordon met the F-4 for the first time, he was struck by one singular impression: the jet was huge! Walking around the McDonnell Douglas Phantom II on the blazing concrete ramp, Harry was amazed that a warship this big had been constructed to carry just two fliers. But then again it had actually been designed to carry something much different from the two aviators who controlled the beast. It was built to carry weapons, lots of weapons.

The F-4D could carry the war to the enemy. The Phantom was a flying war store. It could carry anything from light harassing antipersonnel munitions to the the big ones that can end a war or a world. The exhaust ports of the twin GE afterburning turbojets were as big as caves and when the JP-4 poured in and was ignited by the afterburners, they looked like twin entrances to the heart of hell.

Harry had been trained to feed the monsters of aerial combat. He had already been in-country for almost a year, fitting other aircraft with weapons. This would be his first experience with the 4. He looked forward to the challenge.

The F-4 had been developed for the Navy as a carrier-based, multirole attack aircraft. At first the Navy was not impressed. Even the men who fly it know that the Phantom is not just another pretty face. But when it started beating the snot out of the Navy's best fighters, the brass started to take note. When the Air Force got a look at the Navy's new toy, they just had to have some. In fact, the Tactical Air Command immediately replaced over half of its fighter force with F-4s.

It was called the most versatile combat jet in the American arsenal. And now Harry was going to get to work on the best.

It wasn't going to be easy. In these hectic days of the buildup in Southeast Asia, things were changing almost too rapidly to keep up. The brass kept throwing more and more tasks at the F-4s and their drivers. New weapons were hitting the ramp still wet from the drawing board. New roles for airborne platforms like the Phantom were being dreamed up almost daily by the half-mad planners in the dark world business. The crews didn't know what to expect next.

Harry had heard a couple of pilots discussing weapons on the bus back from the flight line. They were incredulous.

"I mean it. When I looked under the wing, somebody had stuck a big green thing with a four-foot daisy cutter on my bomb rack. It had candy stripes all around the ass end. And the crew chief didn't know what it was either. He just told me I better stay away from it because he heard it growl. I didn't know whether to drop it or take it out for a walk."

Harry had chuckled but he knew that it was even more of a problem for the munitions maintenance types. They sometime got tech data for the strange new weapons that were stamped "experimental." It didn't give you a warm fuzzy feeling about handling the bombs.

Harry quickly settled into the normal routine of the new base and new aircraft. It was easy because there was nothing normal about it. They seemed to be making it up as they went along. Everyone got to know everything about all the jobs in his shop. They were called upon to do things that they had never imagined. They never got bored. Every day brought some new job, some new challenge, or some new problems. They put in hours that would have been backbreaking if they'd had the time to notice. But they didn't. They worked through their shifts and into the next.

They were doing vital, exciting work in the middle of a war. They were inventing, doing things that had never been done before. The adrenaline rush kept them from noticing how overworked they really were. It was like the ancient Chinese curse. "May you live in interesting times." These were certainly interesting times.

It was a time of heavy hardships. War always is. The youngest, the best, the smartest could suddenly be ripped from the scene. Death was a constant reminder of the seriousness of the game. But it was also a period of unequaled camaraderie. Shared adversity can do that to a group of people. Everyone was working hard and everyone knew the importance of the others' jobs. In such times of critical peril generated by war, you learned to respect the people who helped you. What it came down to was that your butt was constantly and literally on the line. Everyone had to pull together so that everyone could go home in one piece.

The long hours that Harry and his coworkers were putting in and the ingenuity that they used every day was being recognized by more people than just his supervisors. The crews who flew the F-4s that they loaded and the people who commanded those crews knew what a great job their weapon types were doing. That was it exactly. They started to think of the hardworking weaponeers as "their weapons guys." The brass took a real sense of pride in their accomplishments. The flyers saw evidence of the great job the weaponeers were doing in the most critical situations. The bombs came off the racks and exploded on impact with the pilot-killing SAM sites. The missiles came off the rails in the most violent, last-ditch maneuvers and sped off to home in on the bad guys and bring them to justice. And the racks did not jam and the rails did not lock to endanger the warrior and his bird when they limped back home from the fray.

The powers-that-be noticed this. They noticed that the targets were getting destroyed. They noticed that the enemy was getting less and less anxious to engage their fighters. And they noticed that more of their young warriors were returning to their bases to fight another day.

They noticed and they went out of their way to show their gratitude. Every chance they got they were around Harry and his friends, shaking hands, slapping backs, and buying drinks. They always had time to answer questions and stay after a flight and help solve problems. They remembered names and faces. And they thought of ways to recognize and reward the superhuman efforts of all the people who worked behind the lines in the war effort.

At the base where Harry worked, the commander spent much time talking to his people. He had learned a lot about them. And he had learned an amazing fact. Many of the young men who worked so hard for the air war effort had never themselves flown in an airplane other than the airliner that brought them to the war. This was unheard of to the colonel. He had grown up flying. He lived to fly. He thought that the greatest thing a man could do was to strap on a big jet, like the F-4, and swoop into the skies.

The colonel was a man who could get things done. He resolved to do something about this situation. He had to show his people some of the good things about the flying business. He called in his flight leaders and then he called in the commanders of all the support squadrons. He proposed to them a reward system for their workers. When they singled out a man or woman for duty above and beyond, in addition to the medal or certificate that was the usual reward, the colonel and his men would add something. If the honoree liked, the commander would provide a ride in one of the company war birds with a seasoned fighter pilot.

The word spread like wildfire through Harry's squadron. Men who were tasked to the maximum now worked harder. Everyone wanted a chance to slip the surly bounds of earth in the Air Force's best fighter. Harry felt the same. He worked with the goal in mind for the next week. Then work drove it out of his mind.

Harry was assigned to start arming the big jets with a new generation weapon, a so-called smart bomb. The Air Force didn't like that term. It seemed to imply that the rest of their munitions were dumb. But the bomb looked smart. It seemed to intimidate by its obvious technical sophistication. Harry sweated over the specs for the new bomb. He learned everything he could through long hours of study. Then he spent even longer hours briefing the crews on how the weapon worked. They listened to Harry. He quickly became their expert. And when they finally took the new "smart bomb" out to introduce it to the war, it worked better than advertised.

When they rode back to the base after employing their smart friend, they couldn't stop talking about it. How the weapon swept through the jungle, avoiding the wrong points and finding the target. How it actually flew into the mouth of a cave and eliminated a cache of weapons that Charlie had stored inside.

And when the shouting was done, they remembered Harry. The crews themselves put him in for a medal for all his long and hard work to arm them with this wonder weapon. They saw to it that the paperwork went through as fast as possible. And they carried the orders to Harry themselves.

Harry was amazed that they had gone to this trouble. He was embarrassed by all the attention over someone just doing his job. But when they reminded him of the added bonus that went with the medal, Harry couldn't contain his glee. Finally he would get to blast off in the backseat of a supersonic Phantom.

The day of his flight dawned on perfect weather. Harry

was up and ready a full two hours before he was to report to Base Operations. He hung around the windows to the flight line, cheering inwardly every time an F-4 climbed out on the end of a bright blue flame.

"Hi, Harry, I guess I'm your chauffeur for the day."

Harry swung away from the window and promptly tripped over his own tongue. The speaker, the pilot assigned to take him up on his reward flight, was none other than the vice wing commander.

"Yes sir, I guess sir, thank you sir." Harry saluted so hard he almost hurt his forehead. The colonel put him at ease immediately and headed him out to the flight line. On the way to their designated jet, he talked to Harry about the operation of the weapons shop. Harry was amazed to find out just how much the old man new about the operation. By the time the colonel helped him strap into the fighter's rear ejection seat, Harry felt as though they were old friends.

With the cockpit canopy closed the sound of the big jet was totally different on the inside. It was rumbling that you felt more than heard. Even taxiing out to the runway was a thrill. Harry waved to a weapons crew as they drove by, not realizing that the helmet and oxygen mask he wore were a perfect disguise.

As they lined up on the runway, Harry glanced around his cockpit. The area was covered with strange gauges, instruments, and switches. He was being very careful. He didn't want to accidently touch anything that could blast him and the pilot out of the plane. He watched the pilot in front of him turn and query with a thumbs-up. Harry smiled and returned the thumbs-up gesture. He was ready for the best ride on the midway.

Harry watched over the colonel's shoulder as he flipped a

switch and advanced the throttles. He heard the tower instructions over the radio receiver in his helmet. They were
cleared for takeoff.

The noise increased and then the afterburners roared. They
didn't explode like those of the F-105. They just snuck up on
you until the whole world seemed to be vibrating in reso-
nance with them. Then the pilot popped the brakes loose and
the jet leaped forward.

Before he could breathe or think, the huge warplane was
airborne. Harry felt the acceleration like a giant hand pressing him deeper and deeper into the seat.

"How you doing back there, GIB?"

It took a minute for Harry to remember that he was the
GIB, the guy-in-back. It took a couple of more minutes for
him to remember to talk. When he did he could only stammer out "Great!" Wonderful. Here he was getting the biggest
thrill of his life and he sounded like a cartoon character sell-
ing breakfast cereal.

But the colonel just laughed and said, "Okay, hold on to
your socks."

Harry stiffened as the world suddenly tilted to the right.
For an instant he felt that he was going to fall out of the aircraft. Then, as they rolled past sideways toward inverted, a
funny thing happened. Harry started to like it. This time he
was much more articulate when he spoke to the colonel.
Over the interphone he calmly and clearly stated, "Wheeuh!"

Time flew as they flew. The commander put the big jet
through its paces and seemed to be having as much fun as
Harry. He was delighted that the young man was enjoying all
the radical maneuvers. He pointed out the beauty of the jungle from the sky. It was a different world when they flew

over it rather than walked on it. Then, much too soon, it was time to head for the base and the mundane earth.

They flew over the runway too high to land. The colonel explained that it was part of the routine to get clearance to land. The tower answered their radio request for landing and the colonel banked the jet sharply to the right. As they headed back to line up for a landing, the colonel was telling Harry that he thought he must be a born flyer. He was in the middle of a sentence when he stopped abruptly.

Harry was looking at the runway from above and abeam it so he didn't notice at first. He looked up and saw that the colonel seemed to be slumped to the right. His helmet rested against the canopy window.

"You okay, sir?" he asked over the interphone.

There was no reply. The F-4 sailed calmly ahead. The stick between Harry's legs remained steady. It was tied to the colonel's controls and mimicked his every move.

Harry tried to talk to the colonel again and again received no reply. *Maybe the interphone is broken,* he thought. He recalled the abrupt way the colonel's voice had stopped right in the middle of a sentence.

The colonel's head continued to rest against the window and seemed to rock gently with the motion of the jet. They passed far beyond the end of the runway. Harry was about to try and reach the colonel with his hand to see if everything was all right when the stick moved to the right and the F-4 banked gracefully to return to the runway.

Harry knew that landing was the most critical phase of any flight. Pilots had explained that the jet that flew so well in high-speed combat was a real handful to land. It didn't go slow gracefully. Harry didn't want to bother the colonel while he was making all the careful adjustments to the controls to bring them safely back to earth. He sat back and watched the show.

They seemed to glide down final approach. The pilot's touch was so good that they were rolling down the runway before Harry knew they had landed.

The roar of the big jets receded as they coasted to the end of the long concrete strip. The colonel guided them expertly off the taxiway at the end of the runway. Harry watched as his pedals went to the floor as the colonel pressed his to lock the brakes. The Phantom came to a complete stop. Harry's dream flight was over. It was now one of his favorite memories. He waited for the colonel to turn and tell him how to climb out of the big bird.

But the colonel didn't turn. He didn't move. He sat slightly forward in the seat with his head resting against the cockpit glass.

Harry waited and waited. Then he grew anxious. He pulled off his flight glove and fiddled with the parachute harness. He finally freed the chest strap enough to reach forward and touch the colonel's shoulder. One touch told him something was wrong, dreadfully wrong.

"Hey, Colonel, hey sir, what's wrong?" Harry shook the colonel. There was no response. The vice commander remained where he was.

Harry started to panic. He was sitting in a jet with the engines running and the hatch closed and he had no idea how to open the door or call for help.

He looked frantically around the cockpit, trying to find something that looked like a radio switch. He was afraid to touch anything. Somewhere in that maze was a switch that would send him rocking out in the ejection seat. He heard the tower ask if anything was wrong and he heard another voice.

It took him a while to realize it was his own voice. He was babbling, trying to wake the colonel, trying to find the switch. Finally he got enough courage to press the button by the throttle switches.

"Hey help. Something's wrong with the pilot. I'm stuck in this F-4 and I can't get the colonel to wake up. You better send for a doctor or get an ambulance."

"Okay, friend, just sit tight. Help's on the way." The tower message in his radio receiver was like the word of God to Harry. "Oh, and maybe you better not touch anything until they get there," the angel added.

Harry sat on the raised bed in the doctor's office. He couldn't stop shaking. He didn't really feel the needle when the medic gave him the shot.

"Hang in there, buddy. This'll make you feel a whole lot better. Really good drugs."

Harry smiled a weak smile. He felt a warmth spreading from his arm and he seemed to be able to control his shivering a little better.

"You must be some natural pilot. The tower guys said you made a perfect landing. Just like a pro. You must have had some lessons or something, huh?"

"What are you talking about?" Harry looked at the young intern in confusion. "I didn't land the plane. The colonel did."

"Uh-uh. Couldn't have. Doc said he was dead long before touchdown. Must have been a really severe heart attack. You should have seen his face. We didn't even know it was the vice commander until we checked his ID. He had to have been dead for about twenty to thirty minutes."

In spite of the drug coursing through his veins, Harry

started to shake again. All of the blood drained from his face. The young medic was startled.

"Hey somebody give me a hand here," he yelled. "This guy's going into shock."

Well, yes, Harry thought as strong hands laid him on the bed. *I guess it is shock. But it's probably a different type of shock than they think.* It was the shock of recognition. Harry had just realized who had landed his airplane.

The colonel must have earned another set of wings . . . in another kind of air force.

SCHOOL SPIRIT

I'VE *been through combat and flight training and long
late missions in an old aircraft in bad weather but none
of these experiences ever affected me as much as trying
to help out in my wife's preschool class. She's a good
teacher. Hell, she's a great teacher. Just ask her students.
Some of them may be a little more difficult to communicate
with than others. But she seems to get through.*

There are many things that abound on military bases.
Everyone knows they have a lot of weapons. They also have
a lot of cars and trucks and aircraft and tanks. Bases have a
lot of signs and fences and locked doors. And they have a
whole lot of serious, efficient men and women in many different uniforms.

But military bases also have a lot of something else that

you may not have thought of. They have a whole lot of children.

Believe it or not, military kids, or military brats as they refer to themselves, are really a lot like kids everywhere. They go through the same feelings and foibles and fads that civilian kids do. They're just like the kids on any block, with one difference. They have probably been around a whole lot more blocks than most kids.

Military kids learn a few things that others kids don't get exposed to. They learn that you never write your friend's address in your book in ink. They learn how to memorize a new phone number in record time. They learn how to find their way back home even if they aren't sure exactly what home is. They learn how to avoid the new kid syndrome or at least how to get over it quickly. They can learn a new teacher's name, a new street number, and a new zip code with relative ease. And they learn that you don't die from being homesick.

When a person enters the military, he is told time and time again that you have to be flexible to get ahead. But it's the kids who really learn the lesson. And they have to learn to be flexible not just to get ahead but to survive.

This is not to say that military people treat their kids poorly. Quite the contrary. The military family goes out of its way to provide for its children.

When it comes to education, the military is in the forefront of involvement and innovation. The modern military has discovered the importance of education. And as the mothers and fathers in the military come to understand how important education is for themselves, they can easily deduce how important it is for their children.

They demand only the best for their kids, and in most

cases the military is happy to oblige. When kindergarten classes were not mandatory, they were available on military bases. Now that preschool education is considered optimum but not mandatory, military bases go out of their way to provide preschool for military kids.

Minot Air Force Base in upper North Dakota was such a base. It was isolated by both distance and extremes of weather. It was not regarded as a dream assignment. And it gave the Air Force a real chance to shine. If the brass could make Minot a comfortable base for its working families, they would have really accomplished something. And they did. It became a good place to live. When it came to schools, the base excelled. North Dakota was proud of its high rating in the education of its young people. The air base schools continued the tradition.

When the best minds in education stressed the need for an early start in school, the base was right there to establish a well-equipped and modern preschool.

Base schools benefit from a resource that is often overlooked by outsiders. Husbands and wives of well-educated professional military personnel tend to be likewise well educated and professional. Many are teachers with a wealth of experience to draw on. They become the core of teachers for the base schools. Such was the case for the new preschool.

A dedicated and knowledgeable staff was chosen and presented with the task of turning a former office building into a four-star preschool. The task was not too difficult. The building was large with several spacious rooms. It had been used for many purposes in the past and had amenities that preschools didn't usually offer. The base provided as much support as it could squeeze from the budget and the dedicated teachers and their spouses provided even more.

In no time the preschool became a reality. One class grew to two classes that split to four classes that led to morning and afternoon classes and on to a waiting list and an obvious need to enlarge the drawings of the proposed permanent facility.

The teachers worked hard to make the school the best in the area and it became a magnet for base parents. And as the hardworking teachers found out, the building became a magnet for something else.

Preschool teaching looks like an easy job. An outsider would look in and see what appears to be an adult playing with the kids. The classroom is a cheery place to work and the classes usually only last two to three hours a day. Nothing but fun and games.

But nothing could be farther from the truth. Ask the husband or wife of a preschool teacher. They'll tell you how much hard work and time goes into teaching the little ones.

The teachers of the Minot Air Base preschool worked long and hard to make their program the best. It was not unusual to drive past the school early in the morning or late at night and see the lights on. The janitor would invariably find one or more teachers still hard at work when he got there in the evening. And more times than not they would still be there when he left at night.

The first hint that the school might house more than the registered students came one night while a teacher worked in her room to change a bulletin board. She had found some brilliant prints from a publication about exotic fish and was anxious to share them with her class. The janitor had said good-night over an hour ago and she was alone in the building. Or so she thought.

As she worked, she became aware of a feeling that had

slowly intensified. She couldn't put her finger on it but it was an uneasy kind of feeling that made her lose her concentration. Slowly, bit by bit, she realized what it was. Someone was watching her. She couldn't see anyone and she couldn't hear anyone, but the feeling persisted. Someone was watching her. It was that prickly feeling you get on the back of your neck when you know someone is staring at you from behind. She caught herself several times, jerking her head around to catch the voyeur. But of course there was never anyone there.

It was silly, she knew. Must have worked too hard, she told herself. Silly. But the feeling kept getting stronger and stronger until she finally found herself just watching and no longer working.

She resolved to do something about it. She would tour the building. If she could convince herself that there was no one else on the premises, maybe the feeling would go away.

She went from one end of the building to the other, checking each classroom and every closet and storeroom. Just as she had known before she started, there was no one here but her. All she found was a light that the janitor had left on in the office. She turned the light out and locked the office door while she puzzled over the strange feeling. Where had it come from?

She felt better until she reentered her classroom. Suddenly she was overwhelmed by an even stronger feeling of being watched. It was overpowering and suffocating. She couldn't handle it. She grabbed her coat and rushed from her room. The minute the door was shut, the feeling went away. Her pounding heart stopped racing and her breathing slowed. And, of course, she felt silly again. But she didn't feel like going back in the room. Not that night.

As she walked to the front of the building she noticed that the office room light was on. She thought she had turned it off but she must have been mistaken. How funny. She had locked the door but left the light burning. Must be more tired than she thought. She turned the light out and relocked the door.

She locked the outside door of the school and started for her car. As she turned from the building she heard a sound. It was indistinct but still recognizable because she heard it so often during the day. It was the sound of a child giggling. She wanted to turn back to the building and search it once again, but she kept walking resolutely to her car. She resisted every impulse to turn and look at the building, afraid of what she might see. She started the car and put it in gear, then, without thinking, glanced in the mirror at the building. She saw nothing—nothing but the light in the office.

Several days later, the secretary arrived early to unlock the building. She was as dedicated as the teachers, handling many jobs that were not normally part of the job description for a secretary. As she opened the door she heard a sound that can send chills through a school worker. It was the sound of running water. Somewhere in the building a tap had been left on full blast. She raced through the building, with thoughts of flooding and damage haunting her mind. As she opened each door she just knew that the water would be on behind it. But she couldn't find the source of the sound.

Several times, as she made her panicked inspection of the building, she heard faint laughter. It was as if someone, someone young, was amused by her distress. She searched the building from top to bottom but was unable to find the expected waterfall. Finally she stood in the office, listening to the water cascade, somewhere. She was about to call the civil engineering office, when the front door opened. The morning teacher walked in.

She ran to her.

"You hear that? You hear the water? Where do you think that's coming from?" she blurted out.

"Hear what? I don't hear anything."

The secretary stopped. She listened hard. There was absolutely nothing to hear. The phantom water leak had stopped abruptly with the entrance of the teacher.

In spite of a lack of evidence, she did call CE. They went over the building and under the building and checked all the pipes and valves and finally left muttering about hysterical women. They had found nothing.

As the days passed, and the year waned into winter, each teacher and worker in the preschool found something unusual about the building. The classrooms, so filled with light and sound and joy by day, became strange, uneasy places at night.

One teacher became accustomed to the sound of running and skipping feet in the hallways as she worked in her room. Several investigations had yielded no human origins of the sounds.

Another teacher learned to look for small items from her desk and tables in the most unlikely places. She found that if she thought first where her pencil or key ring shouldn't be, it was usually there. It was as if someone was playing a nonstop game of hide-and-seek.

The secretary learned to disregard the sound of rushing water so well that when a hydrant broke outside the building she didn't investigate until an excited parent rushed in to tell her to call the fire department. The parking lot was being flooded. As she dialed the number, she heard childish laughter that might have come from one of the classrooms, but didn't.

Even the security police were the victims of the unknown agency. They reported the lights on in the building so many times that finally they stopped notifying anyone. They must have assumed it was normal for a preschool.

But the strange occurrences had one striking feature in common. They always happened when only one person was in the building. They never took place when there was more than one witness to verify the hauntings. So, because they weren't the kinds of things that people would admit to without verification, each person thought that only she was suffering from a bad case of ghosts. And nobody wants to admit to her friends that she's that far around the bend. It came out quite by accident.

One of the overworked and underpaid teachers was gathering up her homework to leave for the day when she suddenly realized that tomorrow was a new month. A new month meant new bulletin boards and new pictures and new calendar symbols. A new month meant a whole lot of work.

As she settled back in for a long night of work, she said to the empty room, "Okay, ghosts, hope you brought a lunch. Looks like we're in for a long one."

A passing teacher heard her and stuck her head in.

"What did you say, about the ghosts?"

"Nothing . . . nothing at all." She was embarrassed. "I was just talking to myself out loud."

"No you weren't. You were talking to the ghosts. You know about them too. Thank God, I thought I was going crazy."

They finally sat down and compared notes. They couldn't contain themselves. It was like a dam had burst and all the solitary haunting experiences spilled out. They became more and more eager to relate their ordeals to each other and their voices became louder. Before they realized it, the room was filled with all the teachers and workers. And they were all relating similar nightmares that had plagued them. And as they talked about the hauntings and frights, the experiences became less frightening and less shocking. The night seemed to lose some of its power. They proved once again that shared adversity is much easier to take.

And as they talked of the ghosts that haunted their beloved school, they slowly came to the conclusion that the entity or entities that haunted the preschool were not evil spirits. Far from it. Each and everyone of the school workers had been frightened and startled by the happenings but had never felt physically threatened by the presence. In a way they each subconsciously knew that the hauntings were caused by someone who wanted to scare but not hurt. These experts all knew in their hearts that the culprit, whatever else he might be, was also a child. And they were experts at dealing with children.

So the teachers went on being teachers to the best of their ability. And if they knew that their classes had a few more pupils than showed in the enrollment records, well, they were used to the load.

And they hoped that their ghostly charges were learning right along with their more ordinary schoolmates.

After all, everyone loves to scare the teacher.

MISSED APPROACH

*M*Y first job in the Air Force was that of air traffic controller. It was a hectic, fast-paced life but there were moments, usually in the early morning hours, when we had time to sit back and look around. Pilots have those quiet times to look around and reflect. Sometimes controllers and pilots see things. But you never hear about it. It's just like in the movie, Close Encounters of the Third Kind. Nobody wants to go on record. But something is out there in spite of the record.

Senior Master Sergeant David L. Korta peered through the glass wall of the control tower. The lights of the cab were turned down low to keep them from reflecting off the glass and obscuring the view, but it still took practice to look around the reflections and see what lay beyond. The early seventies was a time of rapid advancement in the technology used to control air traffic, but the tower controllers' main instrument was still a keen set of eyes alertly scanning the horizon. "Brite" radar displays, a combination of radar and computer technology, were being introduced into the tower environment, but few old-head controllers trusted them. You had to really see the traffic to know how to separate it.

Davey Korta had just turned forty and although parts of his body were noticing the march of time, his eyes were just as sharp as ever. Just now he was using them to survey a dimly lit spectacle that never failed to draw his attention. Most military bases have limited numbers of aircraft. A base might be home to fifteen or twenty tankers or bombers or maybe thirty or forty fighters. Add to that a couple of utility birds and maybe a dozen or so helicopters, depending on the mission of the base, and you had the usual total.

But there was nothing usual about Davis-Monthan Air Force Base. Sprawling in the desert south of Tucson, DM was home to a unique facility. The facility was known by official designations that changed with each philosophy upheaval that shook the military. The current official moniker was the Military Aircraft Storage and Disposition Center, but since its inception the place had been known by everyone as the Boneyard.

When it came to airplanes, the services were like eccentric pack rats, seldom throwing anything away. For a time after World War II, the gates of the Boneyard were opened to private investors. The stock of war birds was too great for even the military to think of keeping and storing. But during the earliest rumblings of the police action in Vietnam, the gates were soundly locked and no further aircraft were sold to the general public.

Sergeant Korta looked out over row after row of aircraft lined up within the confines of the huge storage lot. The dry desert air was perfect for preserving the aging aircraft and thousands of them now lined the acres of the Boneyard. There were bombers, tankers, fighters, trainers, and cargo craft. They included the biggest and smallest, the widest and fastest, and, in some instances, the strangest military planes ever built.

Davey could see a disc-shaped radar that shadowed the back of a Navy radar plane like a giant saucer hovering for a landing. Another one in the same row sported an antenna on the nose that looked like the plane had been run through with a rocket.

Finally he pulled himself away from the contemplation of the elephant graveyard and turned back to the cab of the tower. He took a sip from his thick black coffee and frowned at the bitter taste. Tower coffee was rumored to be deadly to noncontrollers and he was not about to disagree with legend.

He surveyed the other two members of his crew. As senior controller, Sergeant Korta didn't belong to any specific crew. He was responsible for the training and supervision of all controllers on the base. But he regularly took over different crews to see how they worked together. He had to be dead certain that each and every controller under his supervision could do the job. Air traffic control was one of the most demanding and difficult jobs imaginable. It required constant attention to detail and the ability to think and act instantly. Controllers had to have a mountain of information at their fingertips. Like master chess players, they had to be constantly aware of all the pieces under their control and to think several moves in advance. It was like a game. But it was a very serious game. The controller had to always win. If he didn't, people died.

Davey shook his head in silent amusement. At this late hour of the mid shift his "crack team" looked anything but impressive. Buck Sergeant Silvers, the local controller, was demonstrating his prowess at trash can basketball with old copies of weather reports. His able assistant, Airman Couch, was locked in rapt concentration, studying his microphone as it dangled suspended from his limp wrist.

Oh well, thought Sergeant Korta. *Time to shake up the troops.*

"Sergeant Silvers."

The young sergeant bolted upright as Korta's voice rolled across the tower cab like thunder.

"I assume you have completed the traffic count log for the last three hours."

"No . . . uh, yes . . . that is, I'm getting on it right away, Sergeant Korta," the young man managed to stammer.

"Good, good. It's gratifying to see such dedication in the younger members of the Air Force." The senior sergeant turned his gaze on the younger man.

"How about you, Airman Couch? Are you dedicated also?"

"Yes sir, I am sir!" He leapt from his chair and snapped to rigid attention.

"At ease, Airman. And please remember to call me sergeant. Sir is a term reserved for officers. I work for a living."

Korta walked slowly up to the young man and smiled.

"Am I right in assuming that your dedication is directed to your studies? I wouldn't want you to have any difficulties passing your annuals."

"Yes sir . . . I mean Sergeant . . . I'm really studying."

To prove the point he grabbed a book from the console and planted his nose firmly between the pages. His look of concentration was so intense that it looked painful.

"Great," smiled the senior NCO. "But while you're studying so hard, who's going to control that aircraft on final?"

In perfect television sitcom fashion, Airman Couch whipped his head in a double take and dropped his book and microphone.

"I don't know, Sarge. I didn't get a handoff from anybody." The young man stared in confusion at the landing lights glowing to the north of the field. The crystal clear desert air, brightly lit by millions of stars, made estimating distances very difficult. It was impossible to determine if the lights were only a mile away or more than ten.

"Okay, what do you intend to do in a situation like this, Airman Couch? You can help him out, Sergeant Silvers." Davey felt the tones of the master teacher slip into his speech.

"Call center and check for inbounds."

"Call approach and check for traffic."

The two responses were the ones Sergeant Korta was looking for but coming as they did on top of each other, they were almost unintelligible.

"Good. You each get two points for the first correct answer. Now if you'd like to try for even more points, you might make those calls sometime before our mystery guest decides that nobody's home and goes away."

Both young men leapt to the task. Suddenly the quiet tower was awakened by the sound of frantic communication.

Sergeant Korta regarded the progress of the landing lights. They seemed almost to hang in midair, suspended over the distant lights of downtown Tucson. The desert air could play some strange tricks on the eye.

"Center doesn't have a thing," Sergeant Silvers was the first to report. "They sounded like they were mad like I woke them up or something."

"Probably did," observed Davey Korta. "How about approach? They have anything?"

"No, Sergeant, they don't have a single inbound." Airman Couch shook his head emphatically. "All they've heard from in the past hour is that guy from the aeroclub. He's been preflighting that light plane for the past hour."

Couch gestured to the old WW2 trainer that sat under a pool of light on the transient ramp in front of the tower. A munificent Uncle Sam had donated the old trainer to the base flying club. It was still being used to train new flyers and, in spite of its gas-guzzling propensity, it was a favorite of most of the instructors.

"Well, then, I guess what we have here is an honest to goodness 'pop-up.' "

"Pop-ups" were pilots who didn't bother to file flight plans but preferred to navigate from place to place by visual see-and-be-seen rules. As more and more air traffic jammed the airspace over the United States, fewer areas were available for the visual flyers. And military bases almost never got visual flight rules traffic. Almost all military flights required a flight plan and clearance. Military commanders did not welcome drop-in guests.

"Great, what do I do with a pop-up?" asked the confused controller.

"I think trying to establish communication with him would be a great place to start, don't you?"

"Oh . . . yeah . . . right." The airman suddenly remembered the microphone lying on the console where he had dropped it.

He quickly flipped up several switches on the console and keyed the mike in his hand.

"Aircraft on final, runway one-two, Davis-Monthan Air Force Base, identify yourself."

All three listened intently to the bank of speakers across the top of the console. They heard nothing but the light background static that continually issued from one of the speakers.

"Try again," the senior controller directed.

"Aircraft on final to runway one-two, how do you hear me?"

Again the query went unanswered.

"Hit him on guard," directed Sergeant Korta. "I'll call it in to approach."

The airman threw the switch for 243.0, the national emergency frequency. His supervisor made a courtesy call to the Radar Approach Control facility located in the basement of the building under the tower. Guard frequencies were constantly monitored by all facilities and every time one in range was used, the controllers would be anxious to know why.

"Okay, Sarge, we'll listen up and see if we can hear anything from your unknown. I thought the guy on local was kidding when he called down. We haven't had any traffic for a couple of hours now."

The senior radar controller was friendly but somewhat dubious about the possibility of airplanes sneaking up on his sophisticated radar array.

"Here goes." The young airman keyed his mike.

"This is Davis-Monthan tower on guard. Aircraft on short . . . aircraft on final to runway one-two, please identify yourself."

Once again three pairs of eyes stared at the lights glowing in the air above the northern desert. It was as if they expected the lights themselves to talk.

"How far out is he, Sarge?" Sergeant Silvers spoke to his chief but continued to stare at the landing lights.

"Can't tell," Korta answered, also without turning from

the window. "It's hard to tell at night. And it's hard to be sure without a hint from radar."

"Almost looks like he's not moving."

Sergeant Korta nodded, then realized how foolish it was to nod to a person who wasn't looking at you.

As if in response, the lights suddenly seemed to brighten and enlarge, as if the mystery aircraft had moved closer.

"Looks like he's on his way." The apparent movement of the aircraft startled the senior sergeant into action.

"Couch, get the light gun. This guy may be radio out. Silvers, get on the horn to Center and see if they might have lost contact with someone."

The chief controller was gratified to see the two young men in action before he finished speaking. They might be young but they were professionals.

The airman pulled the light gun down from the ceiling. The device looked like a short, cartoon version of a cannon. Couch located the aircraft in the sights mounted on top of the ultra powerful signaling device.

"What do you want me to tell him?"

Korta thought for a moment. Several emergency signals were available to the controller. They were made up of three different-colored lights and pilots were required to memorize the meaning of various combinations.

"Give him a steady green. We don't know what his problem is so we might as well clear him to land. I'll alert the sky cops."

Landing on a military base was a complicated procedure. It required permission in writing from the ruling commander. Those who failed to get the proper permission were invariably greeted by the military police's finest, fully armed for any eventuality.

Even before he hung up the alerting phone, the red lights atop the blue-and-white police vehicles started flashing. They converged on the main ramp in front of the tower so that they could go either way down the runways to greet the visitor.

"What's the matter, did I forget to sign my flight plan again."

Sergeant Korta grinned at the voice coming out of the central speaker.

"Lyle, is that you in that Texan?"

"Yep. Thought I'd take the old lady up for a little night instrument training. I know I'm rusty, but I didn't think you'd sic the cops on me."

"Just wanted to make sure you aren't late for work tomorrow." Sergeant Korta recognized the voice of one of his senior controllers, Master Sergeant Lyle Dennis.

"Seriously, Lyle, we could use another set of eyes down there. We've got an unannounced visitor on final to one-two. Let me know if you see anything wrong with him."

Korta turned back to his crew. It was comforting to know that another old head was keeping watch with him.

"What's happening with junior?"

"I've been giving him a steady green, but I'm not getting anything back." The young man pulled his head away from the light gun and contemplated the light. "Shouldn't we be seeing something more than a light at this distance. I can't make out anything about him."

"We should," Sergeant Korta agreed. "Must be a really bright landing light. Looks like he's leveling out for a low approach."

The ball of light slowed its downward motion as it continued forward toward the runway. It moved over the first runway lights. Its own brilliance washed out the strobes at the runway end.

"Couch, keep giving him a light. Silvers, watch to see if he rocks his wings. Everybody look for marking or insignia." Korta gave everyone their orders without turning away from the light.

The bright light reached the concrete of the main runway and glided down the center line about fifty feet above it. Its altitude never varied as it made an almost-leisurely low approach.

Korta watched in a detached kind of awe. There was not a sound from the tower cab and the silence was not broken by the visitor. To controllers used to the roar of military jets, the silence was deafening.

Suddenly the aircraft veered from its path down the runway and angled toward the massed ranks of aircraft in the Boneyard. It seemed to hang suspended over a column of Korean War–era fighters as if in contemplation of the silver jets. Then, just as suddenly, it returned to its outbound course beyond the end of the runway.

"Did you see him rock his wings?" Sergeant Korta was the first to regain his voice. Rocking your wings at the tower was the universal signal for radio out.

"What wings?" Sergeant Silvers stared in rapt attention at the rapidly dwindling light. "I didn't even see an airplane, much less wings. All I saw was that big damn light."

Airman Couch nodded his head in mute agreement.

Davey shrugged.

"That's what I saw too. But I thought I was just getting old. I wanted corroboration from you juvenile delinquents."

Suddenly several speakers went off at once. The security police all wanted to know what was going on. The fire department, always stationed near the runway, was asking what it was, too. And the speaker in the middle of the console squawked to life.

"Okay, Davey, I give up. What the hell was that?"

"Lyle, didn't anyone ever teach you not to swear over the radio?" answered Davey. Then a thought hit him.

"Lyle, what direction were you filed to fly tonight?"

"South" came the terse reply.

"Do me a big favor if you're up to it. Follow our visitor and see what you can make of him." The senior controller glanced around the cab. "We have conflicting opinions about his make and model."

"Yeah, right, make and model. Well, pass my intentions to approach and clear me for an immediate takeoff. Oh, and one more thing you can do for me, Davey."

"What's that, Lyle?"

"Have the shrink waiting to meet me when I get back. I need to have my head examined."

Davey Korta chuckled at his friend's request. He called down to the approach controllers to let them know what Sergeant Dennis would be doing. The other controllers had answered the rash of radio calls with the verbal equivalent of a shrug, a time-honored military tradition. The consensus of opinion from the ramp tramps was that they were mad at the tower for confusing them. Slowly the flashing red lights departed from the taxiways.

The big reciprocal engine on the T-6 Texan spun the big silver prop to life, and Sergeant Dennis taxied the old yellow trainer to the end of the runway.

"Texan 65 papa, requests clearance for an immediate take-off."

"Sixty-five papa, wind calm, cleared for takeoff, runway

one-two." Sergeant Korta thought for a moment, then keyed the mike again.

"Be careful out there, Lyle."

"Sixty-five papa roger. You got that right, Hoss. I intend to cover my rosy red with both hands."

The subdued tower crew watched until the aircraft disappeared into the velvet blackness south of the base. Now all they could do was wait.

Time and the night dragged with infinite slowness. Suddenly, finally, the silence of the tower cab was interrupted.

"DM tower, this is Texan 65 papa, request clearance for a straight-in runway 30."

"Lyle ... er 65 papa, wind calm, cleared to land." Davey grabbed the mike and transmitted before the other two could move.

"What happened, 65 papa?"

"I'll tell you in person. I don't want this to go down on tape for posterity."

The tower crew could barely wait while the pilot landed the big, yellow trainer and taxied it to parking. They watched him jump out of the plane and walk toward the tower.

The questions started the minute the elevator doors opened.

"What happened?"

"Did you get a good look at the spook?"

"What kind of plane was it."

"Hold it, hold it," Lyle Dennis waved the questioners to silence.

"Let me tell it from the beginning. That way maybe I'll figure it out myself."

The tall master sergeant grabbed a cup of coffee and leaned into his tale. He told how he got airborne, and poured the coals to the old trainer, expecting a long chase to catch up with the mystery plane. He flew down a darkened valley and crested a ridge at the end. As he climbed over the ridge, he was almost blinded by the lights of the other aircraft. It was as if it had been killing time, waiting for him. He throttled back on the power and approached it slowly. It matched his speed and stayed the same distance in front of his craft. When he accelerated, it accelerated. When he slowed, it slowed. It was like a cat-and-mouse game, but Lyle didn't know which one he was supposed to be.

He followed it for several minutes, intent on getting a closer look. He wanted to at least identify the type of aircraft. To him it still looked like a big landing light with no airplane attached.

Suddenly the light seemed to grow in the windscreen. Lyle realized that the craft had come to almost a complete stop. That was impossible. They had been sailing over the desert at better than 130 knots. Now the other was stopped without even a slowdown coast.

"I glanced around trying to figure out what to do. I had to slam it into a forty-five-degree bank to keep from flying right up his tail pipe. Then I noticed that there weren't any lights on the ground anywhere. That SOB had led me out into the wilderness and now it wanted to play.

"I lost him in the bank and figured I was going to live. All of a sudden there he was right next to me, pacing me in wingtip formation. I could have almost reached out and touched him."

"What did you do then, Sergeant Dennis?" Airman Couch was listening to the narrative with his eyes so wide they looked like they were about to drop out.

"I did what any hero-type pilot would do: I shoved the

throttle to the wall, closed my eyes, and screamed all the way home. It's a wonder I didn't run into a mountain or something."

"What happened to the other aircraft?" asked Sergeant Silvers.

"I never saw him again, thank God. I hope I never do."

"Lyle, what did he look like?" Davey was contemplating the unknown with disbelief around the corners of his eyes. "Did it have any markings? Was it military? What did the wings look like? What did the tail look like?"

"Davey, old buddy, if you forget I ever mentioned it, I'll tell you. As far as I could tell, it didn't have any markings. And it didn't have any tail. And as far as I could tell it didn't have any wings. In fact it only had one thing that I'm sure of."

Davey regarded his friend.

"What was that?"

"It had windows. Lots of windows. And if I was to think about it real hard, which I didn't intend to do, I would have to say that there was some kind of eyes behind those windows. Some kind."

It is the position of the United States Air Force that there is no such thing as flying saucers.

It is the position of Senior Master Sergeant David L. Korta that sometimes the United States Air Force is full of grade A, number one horse hockey!

NEVER SURRENDER

T HE military, even more than politics, makes for strange bedfellows. You rarely get the chance to choose even the type of accommodations, much less the people you will share them with. But you learn to adapt. It's easier because usually your roommates are in the same boat. Usually they're military too. Usually they've had to adapt and accommodate to some different situations. And usually the people with whom you share your living spaces are still among the living . . . usually.

It all started in upstate New York, in March, on my roof. I was up there in waist-deep snow, trying to chop the ice out of the gutters, when I got this bright idea. I thought, "I'll bet the South Pacific is nice this time of year."

Yeah, I know, brilliant. So, anyway, the guys in personnel

had been calling around trying to drum up volunteers to go to Guam. I decided to hold up my hand.

Now, I didn't know how my wife would take the idea of living on an island, what with the kid being so young and all. So I got another brilliant idea. I asked her to help me dig the car out of the garage. We had just had a light, spring snowfall of about two feet of the wet stuff.

After a couple of hours of digging, I sprang the Guam idea on her. She was so ready to get out of the winter wonderland that she almost volunteered without me.

Next day, Monday, I called the guy in charge of bomber assignments to ask how soon he can get me to the Pacific.

He said, "Are your bags packed, Captain?"

A real comedian, I thought. But by the end of the week, I had orders in my hand. They were really anxious to get guys over there.

It was the middle of March. The orders were for the first of June. Didn't give us much time, but you'd be surprised how fast you can move with the proper motivation.

We got the house sold, the furniture packed, the movers came, and we took off to California to visit the family before flying off to paradise.

Unfortunately, while we're on leave in California, a young lady pays a visit on Guam. A young lady named Pamela. And she really screwed everything up for us.

See, Pamela is this great big, force 5 or something, typhoon, and she hit Guam real hard.

I found out about it when this personnel weenie called to tell me that my orders had been changed.

I could still go but my family would have to wait until I got assigned a base house.

Well, Grandpa and Grandma were overjoyed that my wife

and kid were going to stay longer. And my wife was happy because she could go shopping a lot more with my mother in L.A. No one shed a tear when I left to "bach it" on an island that had just gotten modified by disaster.

Anyway I spent about twenty-seven hours in this cattle-car airliner and when I got to the island they stuck me in this motel room with no glass in the windows and a fan with one blade missing. They told me they'd get me a house when they got enough of them cleaned up. Most of the houses were still standing, all right. But they were a mess. See, the builders figured that it's easier to dry a house out than build a new one. So they built them to let the wind and water go right on through. No kidding. Some of them even had drains in the middle of the floors.

So, anyway, I spent the next couple of weeks getting settled in the squadron and haunting the housing office every spare minute. Finally, I asked one of the women if I could at least look at a house to see what they're like.

She handed me this key to a place and told me not to expect too much 'cause they hadn't gotten around to cleaning or painting it.

I went to see it expecting the worst. But it turned out to be halfway decent. Oh, it smelled a little wet and the government furniture was trashed. But it wasn't too bad.

The backyard was different. It butted up to this big hole. Sort of like a two- or three-acre canyon.

The neighbor guy said it was a natural depression that the Air Force decided to use as a drainage ditch for things like typhoons.

He said that during the storm it filled up because some garbage blocked the drain. Some idiot swam out to try and clear it out. He must have done a good job because it emptied out real fast. But the guy got sucked right down with the water and they never found him.

He also told me that the house I was looking at was one of the least damaged. His place right next door got wasted. I guess typhoons are funny kinds of storms.

So, anyway, I went back to the lady at housing and told her that I'd take the place. She said, "Yeah, right. It'd be a month before CE could get to it."

And I told her that I'd take it just the way it was if they'd throw in some new furniture.

And she said what about the repairs?

And I told her, "No sweat, I'm handy." So I lied. So what. It got me a home.

That night I called the wife back in California and told her how lucky we were and that she could call the travel office and arrange for her and the kid to come to Guam.

She asked about the house. She said she ran into a friend who had been stationed on Guam who told her about the houses. She said to be sure to get a Capeheart model because they have these neat lanais.

I told her I didn't know about lanais but this house had a kind of an indoor patio that was separated from the living room by glass doors.

She got all excited and told me that that was a lanai. So now I knew what a lanai was.

I went back to the motel next day and picked up my junk and moved into the new place. I figured anything was better than that dump. All I had was my baggage and some ruined furniture, but I could rough it.

It was funny. The stuff in the house got soaked but the patio furniture on the lanai didn't seem to be wet at all. Now the weather on Guam is so good it's almost boring. It's like seventy-five to eighty-five degrees every day of the year and it rains warm water. So I figured, what the hell, I could sleep on the lanai. Sure wouldn't have to worry about getting cold. And the old couch out there looked comfortable.

What a night. I kept dreaming I was waiting for somebody and woke up every twenty minutes. And when I woke up there were these glass doors acting like a mirror right in front of my nose. I scared myself about a hundred times. Finally I decided it must be something about the night air, so I dragged the old couch inside and slept like a baby.

Eventually the furniture got there and my family got there and we set up housekeeping for real. My wife just loved the house and she really liked the lanai. She made that her first job, fixing it all up. Made it look real nice and cozy. But it was funny. Right from the start, even though it looked great and was real comfortable, nobody seemed to want to stay out there very long. There was just something about the place.

Finally the kid sort of inherited it by default. Sherry would tell him, "Take your toys and play out on the lanai." So he would. He started out with all his toys—his cowboys and Indians, his trucks and cars, his spacemen. But before long all he seemed to want to play with was his army stuff. Now, this was kind of embarrassing, me being in the Air Force and all. But the kid was only three years old so no big deal. He even made up an imaginary friend. Blamed everything on him. I thought it was kind of smart of him.

But he never gave him a name. Just called him "he" or "the army man." We'd tell him to play with his cars but he'd say, "He doesn't want to. He just wants to play war." And it was funny. He was only three but when he was playing army with the army guy it wasn't like a little kid playing. It was like real serious. Sometimes he'd be playing and then suddenly he'd stop and come in. Said the army man didn't want to play anymore.

Finally, he quit going out there altogether. Gave Sherry some story about how the army man was sad and didn't want to play much. Sherry didn't push it because she started to have a thing about the lanai herself.

See, she'd always had this kind of thing about places. It's not like she's some big-deal psychic or anything. But she has feelings. Like when her dad was so sick and she knew he was going to die. Nobody told her anything because she was a little girl. But she knew anyway.

And then every once in a while she'd get these feelings about someone she hadn't seen in a long time and before you knew it they'd be calling her or writing to her. It was only a little spooky.

After a while she started to encourage J.T. to play out in the back or in his room. She said that the lanai didn't seem healthy. She wouldn't explain it because it seemed to embarrass her.

I was pulling a lot of alert by this time so I was gone a lot. Sherry started to really develop a thing about the lanai. She said when she sat in the living room sewing or something it always felt like someone was watching her. Someone out on the lanai. It got so bad that on one of my back-to-back tours she went out and got curtains to cover the lanai windows. Said it made the place brighter. Yeah brighter. It also covered up the lanai so nobody could look in on her.

Then it got real strange. First, my mom came over to visit. No, I don't mean there's anything strange about my mom. While she was there, J.T. told her all about the army man. She didn't know that he was imaginary. She didn't know too much about the military. She thought he was talking about some real army guy. So one night she was out in the living room while Sherry was giving J.T. a bath. We tend to be pretty loose on a base. Nobody every locks their doors and it's pretty normal for someone to walk into the lanai so that they can knock on the glass door. Couldn't hear someone knock outside too well.

Anyway, she came and told Sherry that someone was there to see her. Sherry went out but there was nobody. She said, "Where, Mom?" and Mom told her on the lanai. But there was nobody there.

Sherry asked her who it was. Mom said, "I think it was your friend, the army man that J.T. keeps talking about." Sherry got a chill and just stared at Mom. Mom said, "You know, he had on a tan uniform, not like the one Chuck wears."

Sherry just said something dumb like "oh," but she didn't sleep all that night, thinking about J.T.'s army man.

Finally, one night after Mom left, I came home from a real late flight. It was more like real early 'cause it was three or four o'clock in the morning. I went to open the lanai doors and they were locked. We never lock our doors but this time Sherry or somebody did. So I was stuck out there on the lanai without a key. It was like four in the morning and I didn't want to wake anybody up. I knew Sherry would be getting up at six so I decided to wait. See, I'd been flying all night and I wasn't thinking too straight.

So I sat down on the papa-san chair and before you knew it I was dreaming. Or at least I think it was dreaming. It was real strange. It was like I was hearing this story and living it at the same time.

I was on this island but I wasn't me. But I'm not sure who I was. The island was Guam but most of the buildings were either missing or real strange. I was waiting. I was waiting for something to happen. I kept looking up and seeing these airplanes go over. They were up high so I couldn't tell what kind they were. For some reason they scared the crap out of me. I kept thinking Saipan, Saipan. But I didn't know what that meant.

Then all of a sudden the dream got real intense. There were all these explosions and loud bangs. It was like having your head in a bucket with some yo-yo beating on it with a club. It went on and on until I couldn't hear myself think.

I kept running and moving and ducking and hiding but I didn't know from who. There were other guys around me but I couldn't see them very clearly.

Then suddenly I was all alone on this little hill overlooking a big drop-off. It was almost like the drain hole out back but at the time I couldn't place it. All I knew was that I was all alone. And I'd never felt that all alone and lonely in my life. It was so sad that I couldn't take it and I woke up. But I must not have been all the way awake. Because I was staring at my reflection in the glass doors, but it wasn't me. It was this guy in an old dirty tannish kind of uniform. He had some kind of straps wrapped around his shins up to his knees and he had on this pot of a helmet, like nothing I'd ever seen. And he was carrying a gun, an old bolt-action job with a long wooden stock. It looked like it had some kind of flower painted on the stock.

He was standing there staring at me and he had the saddest look I'd ever seen in my life. It just hit me way down deep.

I don't know how long I stood there looking at him. Gradually I realized that he was gone and it was just my reflection. Then Sherry opened the door and I just about jumped out of my skin. Sherry matched my jump because she didn't know I was standing there on the other side of the curtains. Adrenaline—what a rush!

I just couldn't get the dream or whatever out of my mind. I kept wondering who he was and what had made him so sad. I knew deep down that he wasn't some figment of my imagination. He was a real guy.

Then a few weeks later we were knocking around the island, taking in the sights. We were at this little park in Agana. I was enjoying the sun and Sherry took the kid into this little building off to the side.

After a few minutes she came out and she was all white like she'd seen a ghost.

"Maybe you better come in here and see this," she said. "J.T.'s found his army man."

The building turned out to be this little museum about the war on Guam. I saw J.T. standing in front of this glass case looking at some old Japanese army clothes.

"Is that like your army man wears?" I asked him. And he nodded his head. I agreed with him. It was just like the guy I saw in the glass door.

The display was about this guy who was a Japanese soldier who got left on Guam and stayed hidden for sixteen years. He finally walked out of the jungle in 1960, still not convinced that the war was over. I got a copy of the book he wrote. I read it. Then I knew what was going on.

He wasn't the only one to survive and be left. There were a bunch of them. He was one of the few to make it out alive, though.

It was some story. How he and his friends, just kids, got drafted into the army and shipped off to Guam just before the Allies came to take it back.

How they watched the enemy airplanes, our airplanes, fly

over from the south, night after night, day after day. Concentrating on another island, probably Saipan. How they heard the constant bombardment of Saipan in the distance. How they wondered when their turn would come. There was no doubt that the Americans would come. There was little doubt that they would win. But the Japanese had been instructed to fight on, fight for the emperor. Never yield, never surrender.

I read how the bombardment finally started. It went on for hours and days and it was like living in hell. I read how they waited for the invaders to follow the bombardment and kill them all. They waited until they could wait no more and finally the attack came. And their leaders didn't know what to do. There was no orderly counterattack. It was every man for himself. Many finally found themselves alone, cut off, and hopeless.

They didn't know if the war was over. They didn't know if their army had been defeated or had left. They only knew that they were alone and they could not surrender.

That's what I think happened to the guy on our lanai. He got left. He got separated. And then he died. But he never surrendered. And I don't think I would be able to tell him that their army lost. But I wish to God that I could tell him that it's over.

ABOVE AND BEYOND

WHEN I entered the service it seemed to be full of old farts who spent all their time reminiscing about Korea and World War II. As I neared the end of my service it seemed that all the old farts had been replaced by a bunch of young kids who thought Vietnam was ancient history. Yeah, I know it's hard to see the old farts when you are one. But it was a good thing that the generations got mixed. War teaches us a lot of very difficult lessons. Lessons too painful to have to keep learning over and over again. So I listened to the war stories. I hope the kids still do.

"Bullet Flight, turn right heading 262."

"Roger approach, understand you want us to go right to 262. Is that the military right or what?"

The air traffic controller stared at the blips on his radar screen and immediately realized his error.

"Uh . . . negative Bullet, turn left heading 262."

"Okay, that'll be a lot easier, approach."

"Bullet, roger, say altitude."

"Altitude."

"Bullet, say altitude."

"Altitude."

"Damn pilots!" the microphone flew across the console. "Stupid, egotistical jerks, the whole bunch of them."

The controller reached for the mike again, but another hand reached it first. He stared at the hand, then followed it up to the face. It was probably the oldest-looking face he had ever seen in an Air Force uniform.

"Try it this way." The face smiled as the hand keyed the microphone. "Bullet flight, say altitude."

"Altitude," came the monotonous reply accompanied by muffled laughter.

"Roger, Bullet flight, say canceling flight plan."

"Uh . . . negative approach . . . uh . . . we're level at one six thousand."

"See, you just have to know how to handle 'em." The ancient one smiled and dropped the mike back in the young lieutenant's hand.

"Thanks, but who are you, sir . . . uh. . . . Sarge . . . uh." The junior officer stared in bewilderment at the rank on the intruder's collar. It was like nothing he had ever seen before.

"Warrant officer is the proper designation but Red will do just as well. They've been calling me Red since I enlisted over thirty years ago." He ran one hand through his almost nonexistent hair. "Course back then they had a reason to call me Red."

"Okay, Red, nice to meet you." The lieutenant stuck out his hand. "I'm Skip. Like the way you handled that smart-ass pilot. They're all alike. None of them is worth a bucket of warm spit."

"Now there's where I beg to differ with you, Skip. If you can get someone to cover for you, I'll tell you why. If anyone asks, just tell them I'm inspecting you."

"Oh, my God, you're Warrant Officer Garza." The light of panic glowed suddenly in the lieutenant's eyes. "I'm sorry sir . . . ah Warrant . . . I didn't recognize you."

The young officer had heard about Warrant Officer Garza, the toughest inspector on the general's team. They said he was a thousand years old and tough as nails. He was rumored to have given flying lessons to Curtis Lemay.

"Relax, Skip. It's still Red. You're inspection is already over. I've been watching you for the last hour. Don't worry, you passed."

"Whew." The relief in Skip's voice was evident. "Would you like a cup of coffee, or something?"

The officer handed his mike over to another controller and led the way into a small lounge. After the darkness of the control room, the lounge was almost too bright.

"That was pretty nifty the way you put down that jackass in there. This job would be a whole lot easier without pilots."

"Sometimes they can be a real pain in the posterior," the old aviator agreed. "But I still think that they're some of the greatest people around. Owe my life to several of them. One more than most."

"Oh, I see," replied Skip. He had just noticed the wings that Garza wore over his right shirt pocket. "I guess you would owe a lot to your own pilot. You were a gunner, right?"

"Yes, I was a gunner. On several different types of aircraft. And I served with some very good pilots. But I wasn't talking about my own pilot. I was talking about a different kind of pilot altogether. A fighter pilot.

"Since you just passed your inspection with flying colors and you've got a lot of time on your hands, I'll tell you about him. That is if you want to listen to the ramblings of an old war-horse."

The old gunner didn't wait for a reply. As he wrapped himself in his tale, Skip watched enthralled. It was as if time was unwinding from the old face. He seemed to get younger as he talked about a younger time for the Air Force.

When the war came along I was already in what some youngster would call my middle years. I had been born on a small farm and lived and worked the same one for most of my thirty-two years. I took over after my daddy died and raised crops and a family.

I guess I could have hung around and bought a couple of war bonds while the younger men fought the war, but it just didn't seem right to me. It wasn't some police action like you got going now, with everyone not too sure who's right or wrong. It was easy to choose up sides. That German fanatic with the toothbrush mustache was a real threat to my way of life. So I went down and volunteered. Told the guys in charge that I was only twenty-four. Now I know I didn't fool anybody. But they needed as many men as they could get and I was in pretty good shape so they let me in.

I had every intention of being a pilot. Thought if they gave me a good plane, I could get the war over that much faster. But at the time what they needed most of all was gunners. Way they explained it to me, the B-17 only had seats for two pilots but it had room for eight gun aimers. Being a dumb old country boy, I agreed that it seemed the way to go.

Before I discovered the error of my ways, I was in the middle of a very hot war and up to my elbows in shell casings. Being a gunner on a 17 was a whole new way of life. It meant sitting in front of an open hole in a noisy airplane, freezing to death and wishing the bad guys would show up and try to kill you so that you could have something to take your mind off the cold.

It seemed like as soon as we'd leave Jolly Old England everybody would get mad at us. The air just filled up with nasties who wanted to have our hides. But we did have one or two little friends. They always seemed to arrive about the time things got really tense. They were the proud individuals who flew cover for us.

One in particular was this major who led a squad of P-47 Thunderbolts. The Thunderbolt, or Thunder Jug as the pilots called it, was some piece of work. It wasn't as fast as a lot of the fancier fighters, but boy was it tough.

It was kind of like the cockroach of the air. No matter how many times you stepped on it, it just kept coming back for more.

Everyone on the crew got to know the major. He always showed up when everything got darkest. He was kind of like our own personal silver lining.

He was known by all the bomber crews as "Dad" because on the radio he referred to everyone as "Son." It was getting to be pretty regular. We'd get jumped by a bunch of Krauts. The pilot would get on the horn and start calling for the cavalry. Then all of a sudden we'd hear that voice of confidence on the radio, "Don't worry, Son, here come the good guys."

The major and his boys'd be all over those Nazis. They

seemed to be coming from all directions at once, with their fifties blasting, just tearing that German sheet metal to shreds. And Dad would be right in the thick of things, leading by example. He was easy to pick out. He had a great big bull's-eye painted on the side of his Jug. It was a joke. It was like he was taunting the Germans, saying bet you can't even hit me when I'm in the center of the target.

Him and his boys were so accurate and deadly that the word got around even among the Germans. More times than not we'd see the Messerschmitts turn tail and run when they recognized Dad and his squad. The worst mission would start to feel like a milk run the minute we found out that Dad would be guarding our six.

Just when it felt like some of us might even survive to terrorize the girls back home, somebody decided to tweak it up a notch to damn serious.

We started to notice a whole lot more senior officers sitting in on our target briefings. They were just falling all over themselves to give us dire speeches about the seriousness of our missions. And there wasn't a smile in the bunch of them. The targets got to be the you-gotta-be-kidding-me variety. What made it even worse was that they started sending us up against the same target area two or three times in a row. If you think the bad guys were mad when we went after their ball bearing plants the first time, you should have been there for the second go-round. They were seriously pissed off.

If it hadn't been for guys like Dad to count on, we would have been highly depressed about the whole thing.

Then came that briefing that topped them all. We knew we were in trouble when we pulled up to the briefing hut. There must have been ten cars with little flags on them. The tail gunner took one look and started to cross himself at about ninety miles an hour. One of the waist gunners, who always professed to be a devout holy terror, started to beg the tail to teach him how to do that.

When we saw our target we all got real quiet. The only sound was the snap of jaws hitting the floor. One pilot, who suddenly looked about ten years old, raised his hand and asked if we wouldn't be outflying our escorts just a bit. He was relieved when the answer was in the negative. His relief only lasted a couple of seconds. The briefer went on to explain that there would be no cover for this mission. It seems that another bomb group was to act as a decoy for us, to draw the attention of the German defenses. All the available cover would ride with this group to make it seem like the real thing. Then he said something that really scared us. "Don't worry, guys, it'll be a piece of cake."

Since military units were first put together, the words "piece of cake" have been used as shorthand for a genuine, gold-plated, no-bull suicide mission. Nobody whistled on the way to work that day.

We took off and quickly formed into the defensive units that made the B-17 so formidable. If it held together, the combat wing left little space for the bad guys to maneuver between the airplanes. Then our massed firepower would hold them at bay. But the Nazis were always thinking up new ways to break up the formations. Even if the formation held together, we got stuck in the worst possible position. We were in the outside tail end charlie position in the high group. Seventeens who flew in this position were known as fighter bait.

As we flew out of the right country into the wrong one, everyone was concentrating too hard to talk. We were straining to pick out those little dots that meant we had company.

We all wanted to believe that the fake by the other bomb group would work, but we didn't dare count on it. That was like believing a weather forecast.

It seemed like the brass had finally called one right. We were already entering Germany without being jumped by a single fighter. Maybe this would be a piece of cake after all. In fact things were going so good that the number four engine decided to take the day off. Without a warning, the big twelve-hundred-horsepower Wright on the outside of the right wing just quit cold. The pilot scrambled to compensate and he and the copilot spent the next ten minutes trying to restart it.

"Well, guys, I knew things were going too smooth," the pilot said. "I think we can make it to the target in formation, but it's going to be difficult to keep up going home."

That was not good news. Stragglers were fair game to any predators around. Our only hope was that the fighters stayed engaged with the decoy bunch.

When the blue sky started to get dirty with the black puffs from antiaircraft fire, we all calmed down a bit. It was a well-known fact that the German fighters stayed out of their own flak fields. It was too easy to get hit by your own gunners. Today it was a well-known fact that somebody forgot to tell the Nazis. They jumped us from all directions at once. They had just been playing possum, trying to lure us into a trap. And it worked. Suddenly the well-kept formation ceased to exist. It was every man for himself.

Our pilot threw the ship in the evasive maneuver known as "go every way at once." It must have been intended to throw the Germans off by making them think we were crazy. And it was working, too. Then the bombardier had to ruin it with those terrible words. "Level out, pilot, target coming up."

The chorus of "are you out of your mind" was interrupted by the pilot.

"Shut up, everybody. Bombs is right. We didn't come all this way just to be a target." He paused for effect. "Besides, Herman the German would never expect us to do something that dumb. Just might confuse him."

We leveled out and the bombardier took control of the ship. Every gun blazed at the multiple targets. It looked like a flying circus. For once it looked like the target might actually be as important as intel said it was.

Just as we hit zero in the countdown and the bombs started to fall away, I saw a bad guy start his run. He was definitely lining up on us. He was coming in low from the left, which was a shame, because that was the way we were supposed to turn. I opened up with my gun and yelled for the pilot to break to the right. The SOB just kept coming. I don't think he even paid any attention to my machine gun blazing away. I watched him squeeze his triggers and at almost the same instant I felt a jolt as the number one engine exploded.

The pilot whipped the big bomber into a tight right spiral away from him but the damage had already been done. The only good thing that happened was that the sudden descent put out the flames. But it didn't save the engine. We had just become a two-engine bomber. A lonely, two-engine bomber. When we broke right and descended, what was left of our defensive formation broke left and climbed.

We were now way out on a limb. We were damaged, slow, and all alone. You could almost hear the sound of the coffin slamming shut.

The pilot eased her around and headed for home. We decided to run low and as fast as we could to avoid as much trouble as possible. But with only two out of four left we couldn't get much speed out of the old bucket.

It felt like the whole crew was tiptoeing, trying in vain to hide from the Germans. It didn't work. I looked high and saw four little specks about the same time that the tail gunner announced that he had five of them heading our way. It looked real grim. The specks just kept getting bigger and bigger until they became angry-looking members of the Luftwaffe. They weren't happy about losing the target and it looked like they were going to take it out on us.

"Where the hell did he come from?" the pilot yelled. A big green monster roared over the top of us heading back toward the Germans.

"If I didn't know better, I'd say that was a Jug," guessed the nav. "But I didn't think they were going to be joining us today. Not that I'm complaining."

Everyone started cheering at the same time. Now they could see the star on the wing that assured them that he was on our side. The Germans were as surprised as we were. It looked like a pack of rabbits suddenly being jumped by a dog. The whole bunch of them scattered, heading every which way. We saw the fifties on the wings of the Thunderbolt open up. One, then two of the fleeing fighters burst into flame and spiraled toward the ground. The Jug seemed to be everywhere at once. Before we knew it he had run them all off and was turning back to check us out. As he flew over and dipped his wings in a paternal nod, the nav yelled over the intercom.

"Hey, did you guys see that? It's Dad."

As soon as he said it I caught a glimpse of the bull's-eye painted on the side of the P-47. So Dad had come out to take care of his prodigal children.

He slipped above us to ride shotgun on the way home. Twice more, we saw the bad guys lining up to jump us as we limped back to the home drone. And twice more Dad jumped them and scared them back to where they came from. I had never seen a pilot fly like that. He seemed to be everywhere at once. He made that Jug do things that the designer never even thought of. It was like watching an air show. But it was an air show that saved our butts individually and collectively.

Finally, as we crossed into Merry Olde England, he whipped the big Jug into a fast pass and dropped off to return to his base.

We limped in and landed on the field to the amazement of all the guys who had gone off and left us. They had surmised that we wouldn't be coming to dinner that night. Everyone wanted to congratulate us and shake our hands for bringing the piece of junk back home. But to a man all ten of us had only one thought in our minds. We headed for the nearest phone to call and thank our guardian angel for getting us back.

It was kind of like the three stooges, or rather the ten stooges, all of us trying to talk on the phone at the same time. Finally the pilot did something that he rarely did. He took charge and ordered us to back off.

He took over the call and finally, from the way he kept saying sir every two seconds, got hold of someone in charge. He started to tell whoever it was that we were calling to talk to Dad. Then he got real quiet. He was able to say "I see" a couple of times and then his face went white and the phone dropped from his hand.

"What did they say? Why didn't they put Dad on the horn?"

"They didn't put him on the horn because they couldn't," the pilot said. His voice was low and quiet and it gave me a chill.

"It wasn't Dad who came to our rescue today."

"What do you mean, it wasn't Dad?" demanded the nav. "It was too. We all saw him. You did too, pilot."

"Yeah, I saw him, but according to his commander it couldn't have been Dad. Dad didn't make it to the combat zone. Dad didn't even make it off the ground. His left gear collapsed on takeoff. He crashed." The pilot stopped and turned away, unable to face us. "The Jug was full of fuel and ammo. It exploded. Dad is dead. He died before we even got airborne."

"That's some story, Red." The young lieutenant took a sip from his cup of coffee, never noticing that it was stone cold. "Who do you think it was?"

"Well, we found out that there sure weren't any of our fighters in the area. They were all busy with the decoy group that didn't fool anybody." The old gunner raised his head from the table and looked into the young man's eyes.

"I think, no, I know, regardless of what happened, that it was Dad. Now I'm not what you would call a religious man and I don't believe in miracles. I don't know how it happened. But I think that Dad saved my bacon that day. And I know nine other old men who will swear to it right along with me.

"You know how pilots are. I'll bet he wouldn't believe he was dead until he got confirmation from higher headquarters. And you know how slow paperwork can get during a war."

DUMB LUCK

I'VE *always heard that there are no atheists in foxholes. I wouldn't know. I've never been in a foxhole. But I know for a fact that all flyers are superstitious. It's because of the uncertainty of war. Every flyer carries some little icon, some little lucky piece. Even if they really don't help, they can't hurt. And maybe some of them do work. Who knows?*

When Larry Rogers came to the war in Southeast Asia, it was a very courageous thing to do. It was definitely a death-defying act. It wasn't the fact that he was going to a police action that had blossomed into a very deadly war that caused all the concern. With Larry, it was the fact that he was traveling alone that increased the danger level to ridiculous heights. You see, Larry was a klutz.

He wasn't just any klutz. He was *The Klutz*. He was a star of klutzdom. He was clumsy, uncoordinated, absentminded, and wholly unaware of the dangers of his surroundings. When he walked through a room, you could follow his progress by the disasters. He seldom tried anything new without hurting himself and any innocent bystander who had the misfortune to bystand Larry.

When Sharon, his wife of one year and several contusions and abrasions, put him on the plane at Travis Air Force Base, it was with severe misgivings. She wasn't really afraid that the war was a threat to her husband. She was more afraid that the airliner was a threat. She thought Larry would probably fall down the boarding ramp and kill himself before he ever got a chance to go to war. In fact, as the aircraft taxied to the runway, she had to turn away. She couldn't bear the thought of all those innocent people so near the danger zone around Larry for so long a time.

When Larry alighted from the airliner in Bangkok, Thailand, he stood at the base of the ramp and breathed in the foreign smell of the place. He stood in a vacant eddy of people departing the aircraft, oblivious to the fact that they were giving him a wide berth to save themselves further injury. He took in this first impression of the ancient country of Siam with a growing sense of pleasure. He was here, in a foreign country, a foreign land. Nobody knew him here. Nobody knew what a klutz he was. Maybe here he could start over. Maybe here he could walk on the earth as a normal person. Maybe here he could be reborn.

The spring in his step and his newfound confidence lasted all the way to the customs shed, where he managed, without any effort, to bruise his shoulder, break the handle from his suitcase, and endanger the lives of two customs agents. So much for the wide-open possibilities of a new country. Larry decided to try to survive all the way to the air base. One step at a time. And little steps at that.

Larry went to look for his ride to his air base. It was located at a former Thai airfield up-country, closer to the combat zone. An NCO who had watched Larry's progress in the customs shack looked at him with something akin to trepidation. The tall, ungainly young lieutenant ambled up to his desk. The sergeant had already talked to two of the passengers who had arrived on Larry's aircraft. He didn't believe it possible for one young man to be such a danger to himself and others but he didn't intend to take any chances. One did not return from a war zone by taking chances with the unknown.

"What can I do for you, Lieutenant Rogers?"

"I need a ride to my duty location," explained the young man. "Here are my orders."

He attempted to extricate a ream of paper from his bulging gym bag. The papers all came loose at the same time flying from his hand and knocking over the sergeant's coffee.

Larry made a grab at the flying papers and impaled his hand on an ink pen. He shook his injured hand vigorously, thereby spraying blood and ink over the few papers that he had missed with the coffee.

The sergeant didn't know whether to try and help or jump into the nearest bunker.

Larry boarded the C-130 Hercules that was to take him to his duty station. He thought that the sergeant in charge of transportation had been extremely nice in spite of the accident. The NCO had gone out of his way to see that Larry got the first available aircraft going out. Now with his gym bag on his lap, he stared at the green of the jungle flowing like a carpet under the starboard wing. Even the throb from his bandaged hand couldn't diminish the excitement he felt to be there.

A few minutes prior to landing, the pilot of the big green airplane came on the intercom.

"For all of you departing at our next stop, I have some good news and some bad news. First the bad. We have been informed by control that Mr. Charles is opposed to our landing you reinforcements at the base. He is at the moment lobbing mortar rounds on the field in honor of your impending arrival. To facilitate your safe exit from the aircraft and to insure that me and my crew spend absolutely the minimum amount of time on the ground, upon landing I will lower the tail ramp. If you will all gather by the ramp, the crew chief will assist your rapid departure when we come to a stop. Our time on the ground will be approximately seven seconds so don't delay your departure. And thank you for flying the friendly skies of Southeast Asia."

"If that was the bad news, what was the good news?" Larry asked the crew chief as he stood at the tail of the aircraft waiting for the ramp to open.

"I guess it must have been that we don't have to get off with you," shrugged the crew chief.

As the wheels thumped down and the ramp started descending, Larry grabbed hold of a strap on the side of the plane and leaned out as far as he could to see what was happening. He turned back to ask what he was supposed to do after he got off the Herky-bird. At that precise moment there was a loud Whomp as a mortar round landed near the side of the runway. The pilot jerked the controls involuntarily. Larry suddenly found out that the strap he had been holding on to was not attached firmly to the aircraft. It was attached firmly to a parachute that was hung not so firmly from a peg on the airplane. It came loose. Larry fell from the ramp. The chute snagged on an antenna. Larry found himself flying outside the aircraft down the runway at ninety miles an hour in the middle of a battle. Those who witnessed the sight knew deep in their souls that someone special had come to Thailand.

The guys at the squadron were actually happy to see Larry. War has a way of putting a real drain on manpower. Every man was needed. Even Larry. They had heard rumors about his method of arrival but were willing to discount the stories as mere wartime exaggeration.

The squadron commander was even happier to welcome Larry to the base. And not just because he was a sorely needed replacement. He had known Larry in the States, had flown with him. He knew that in spite of what he was on the ground, when Larry climbed into an aircraft, he was a pilot. And not just any pilot. Larry was a natural. He was one of those rare aviators who are able to become one with the airframe. He flew by feel. He could feel everything that was happening to his plane and everything that it was capable of. The aircraft became an extension of his body and mind. With Larry at the controls, any aircraft would strive to its full potential and beyond.

It was strange. When Larry entered the cockpit, he became a different person. It was almost as if he was using up all his clumsiness on the ground. Because Larry was never clumsy in the airplane. In fact, he was the opposite of clumsy. He was the best.

The commander had actually asked for Larry to join his squadron of F-105 flyers. The "Thud" was a fast, capable, sturdy aircraft. It was also dangerous, difficult, and a handful to fly. It required constant attention and did not forgive mistakes. Only the best could handle the beast.

The commander figured that if he could keep Larry alive and well on the ground, Larry could do wonders in the air. It was with this in mind that he asked two of his friends, Thai nationals, to keep an eye on the unlucky young flyer while he was a guest in their country. They were only too happy to oblige.

Thailand is an ancient country that learned many centuries ago the secret to winning a conflict. It's called assimilation. Many conquering hordes descended on the fertile country of Thailand. In the short run the Thais won or lost the battles. In the long run Thailand almost always won, through the practice of assimilation. A conquering nation would occupy the country, make rules, dictate changes, demand obeisance to their gods, and remain firm for expected revolt. They would then be amazed to find that all their demands were accepted by the friendly and helpful subjugated locals. It was so easy that they lost their combative edge and slowly but surely attuned to the easygoing lifestyle of the Thais. Soon, it was hard to tell who were the victors and who the vanquished. They had been assimilated.

Suwon and Prayoun were benefactors of this least-painful method of conquest. Suwon was a former farmer from Laos who had migrated to Thailand in front of a flood that decimated his family farmstead. Since arriving in Thailand almost twenty years ago, he had prospered as he never had in his native land. He was now Thai by choice and a practitioner of this gentle art of subversion.

Prayoun was a descendant of another country who had conquered Thailand when it was Siam. His family started as visitors and now were locals. He was the youngest of the two, only five years out of high school. He had studied English so that he could get a job at the air base, the best employer in the town. Suwon spoke a version of English that was at best a pidgin learned from his friendly association with numerous GIs. The two Thais were introduced to their charge in a manner that was familiar to most of Larry's friends.

Larry exited the squadron building deep in thought about his duties in the war and failed to negotiate the front steps. He fell the short distance and landed facedown in the only mud puddle for several hundred yards. He landed at the feet of his two unofficial keepers.

Suwon and Prayoun recognized him immediately. As they helped him to his feet, they exchanged a glance that clearly said that their assignment was going to be more difficult than they had thought.

As the days went by and Larry integrated into the war effort, his abilities in the aircraft started to be well-known. His airman skills were prodigious. As he handled assignments that were increasingly difficult and dangerous, he never failed to achieve success. In fact, he usually exceeded the mission goals. It got to be commonplace to call for Larry when the job looked impossible. He was the complete air warrior.

On the ground it was a different matter. The most impossible job seemed to be the one which had been accepted by Suwon and Prayoun. They went about it with everything they had, but trying to protect Larry from himself was just about a lost cause.

As they grew to know him, they began to respect his courage in the face of disaster. And Larry got to face a lot of disasters. Slowly their respect turned to friendship. Larry had fallen in love with Thailand. He was anxious to learn as much as he could about this ancient and provocative place. He wanted to see everything at once.

The three of them toured much of the countryside. The two bodyguards were more than happy to show off their home to Larry. And Larry never failed to draw a crowd. He had another quality. It seemed that people could sense what a danger he was to himself and his surroundings. And like strangers apprehensive about the wanderings of a toddler just learning to walk, they seemed to want to protect him.

Larry, when prompted, would talk to his new friends about his job. He could describe in detail the difficulties of fighting this most-unusual of wars. And the more they listened to his stories, the more concerned they grew for the safety of their charge. They had heard how good he was in the air, but never having seen him in action other than on the ground, they found it hard to believe. Finally after a lengthy discussion with Prayoun, Suwon decided to do something about their fears.

Suwon left the village early one morning and was gone several days. Larry missed his friend and asked Prayoun about him. Prayoun would only say that Suwon was looking for something and would return when he found it.

Meanwhile, the air war heated up. The squadron's operating area was moving farther and farther north and each mile up the length of Vietnam meant an increase in defenses. Larry continued to amaze. He had an almost-instinctive sense of the battle zone. His wingmen swore that Larry could see each and every round fired at his aircraft. He seemed to be able to pick the safest route to get the job done. He was able to avoid the surface-to-air missiles, the SAMs, with uncanny ease.

But the sheer volume of defenses was even starting to show on Larry. He found it was harder and more dangerous each day to get to the target and get back home. And fewer of his comrades were able to get back home. Those without Larry's skill were the first to be lost. Even the skilled warriors were limping back to base with aircraft barely able to remain in the air. The war was getting serious.

After one particularly grueling mission, Larry was delighted to hear that his friend Suwon had returned. Prayoun said that he would meet them in a local restaurant for dinner.

After dinner, Larry asked Suwon about his travels. His friend said that he had been looking for something, something for Larry. He reached into his pocket and removed a silk-wrapped package. With reverence he unwrapped the bundle and took out a tiny statue. It was a golden statue of a figure seated in cross-legged fashion. The face was unusual. The central feature was an enlarged nose. On the back was what looked like characters in some obscure cuneiform.

Prayoun gasped. "You found one. I didn't think you could."

"What, what is it?" asked the young aviator.

"OK Buddha," smiled his friend. "Number one Buddha. Number one, see."

Larry's eyes slid down from the object to Suwon's arm as he pulled back his sleeve. The inside of his arm was a mass of fresh scars carved deep in the flesh.

"Suwon, what happened? Who did this to you?" Larry demanded.

"I do, I do," Suwon laughed. "Number one Buddha. See."

He pointed, not to the scars but to a patch of skin that was uncut.

"What is this, Prayoun? What does he mean?"

"He means he went looking for a number one Buddha. This is his way to ensure that the Buddha is truly a number one. When he found a likely statue, he would hold it out in his hand and draw his knife across his arm. If the knife didn't cut and his arm didn't hurt, it was a number one Buddha. They are very rare. You see, when you wear a number one Buddha, no harm can come to you. You can't be hurt. Suwon tested many before he found this one."

The young Thai marveled at the little golden statue. It radiated ancient age—that and something else. It was almost as if it had a calming effect on its surroundings.

"I never thought I'd see one. See, even the chain that it is suspended from is different. It was made by the monks from an old, old pattern to honor the number one Buddha."

Larry marveled at the intricate pattern of the chain.

Suwon gestured at Larry and smiled. Prayoun, understanding his friend, slipped the chain around Larry's neck.

"We both want you to have this and wear it when you fly."

They would hear nothing of his protestations.

"You are a good man, Larry, and a good friend. We can't watch out for you like friends should when you fly. So promise that you will wear this Buddha, and we won't worry about our friend."

Larry was overwhelmed by the gift and by the thought. Not being a religious man or one given to belief in the supernatural, he was not convinced of the magical properties of the little statue. But, just the same, he wore the necklace out of loyal friendship. After Suwon's painful test of the other statues, he felt he owed it to his friend. As he walked out of the restaurant, his hand automatically clutching the little idol, he didn't even realize that he hadn't tripped over his own feet or run into a light post.

Larry had no idea that his friends' gift would be put to the test so soon. He quickly found out. Their next mission, to put a bridge out of commission, was north. Way north. In fact it was very near a town that started with an H and ended with a holy shit! The brass had decided that the target deserved a maximum push. Instead of making things better, that kind of mission usually made it harder to survive. It seemed like every time extra effort was used on a particular target the other side knew about it before they got there. Larry knew that Charles would be waiting with any number of surprises. He clutched the Buddha as he flew his war bird across the river.

Five miles from the bridge it seemed like everything came up to meet them. The sky had more metal in it than the ground did. Larry wouldn't have been surprised to see the bridge coming up at him too. He put irrelevant thoughts on hold and channeled all of his mind power to avoiding death and destruction. Instinctively he worked the controls and the Thud followed his commands. He jinked and dived and rolled and swerved—always just at the right time. Several times he saw flashing explosions where he had been only a fraction of a second before. Others were not so lucky. The radio was a cacophony of noise and rage. The staccato commands of the frantic pilots rode over a monotonous warble that indicated some were forced to step from their planes. The warble was activated by ejection . . . or worse. This was a very bad place to get out of the airplane. Few came back from so far north.

But Larry flew through it all. He never doubted that his Thud would bring him home. He flew by feel, by touch. He avoided every piece of scrap metal the bad guys could launch. Together man and machine walked over the carpet of flak and slid through the forest of flame. SAMs seemed to lock on to him momentarily, then suddenly decide to go hunt somebody else. Antiaircraft found better targets just as Larry came within range.

Then all at once the veil of smoke lifted and the target loomed ahead. Things had been running in a kind of attenuated slow motion. Now they revved into high gear. Larry saw the bridge, he saw the bombs go, he saw the horizon tilt as he banked to the south, and he saw the missiles salvo all at once. He also saw that there was nowhere left to go. Four missiles flew by and away from Larry. He didn't see the fifth one. It's always the one you don't see that gets you.

A loud clap of thunder, louder than anything he had ever heard, rang through the aircraft. The plane gained altitude in a way that it never had before. It went straight up. All further sound had ceased for Larry with that one loud clap. But he could see well enough that his bird was in trouble. It told him so. The instruments spoke to him in sign language. Every light that could change from green to red did so at once. Every gauge with movable needles demonstrated that capability. Everything else did everything that it could to indicate that things were bad. Larry held his breath and moved the controls ever so gently. They worked. He glanced through the canopy. They were still flying straight and level. It even looked like they were still heading south.

Now just a few of the indications that Larry had would mean that the Thud was about to depart controlled flight. Taken all together, the plane should have been doing its imitation of a tractor. But it continued to fly. Larry did not question it or his good fortune. He kept very still, did not think, and guided the wounded bird ever farther toward the south.

South was good. Every mile south was one more mile

nearer to good guys. Larry glanced at the instrument panel. Every mile also meant one less mile he had to walk. The only gauge that was still working right was the fuel gauge. And it was only working right so that he could get the bad news. In a very short time his airplane would turn into a paperweight. Thuds do not run without fuel.

Larry scanned the area he was passing over. He seemed to be out of the target area defenses, but the jungle could hide many secrets. Before he could come to any conclusions the airplane came to one for him. It got quiet. Time to get out. Larry wrapped his right hand around the little Buddha hanging on the front of his flight suit and activated the ejection system. His final thought was *Too late; too late*.

Larry woke up on the ground. Cautiously he tried to assess his injuries. One as accident-prone as Larry was used to the routine. He was amazed to complete his inventory with purely positive results. He could find no broken bones or open wounds. He didn't even have a headache. Then he saw something that chilled him to the bone. He was lying right next to the wreckage of his recently vacated flying machine. It was incredible. Even low on fuel it should have burned on impact. Larry would have burned too, sucked by the draft into the fireball. But there was no fireball. He looked at his tightly clenched fist. It was wrapped around the little Buddha. He opened his hand and stared at it. "Did you have something to do with this?"

He suddenly realized that he needed to be somewhere else fast. The wreck was sure to draw a crowd. He shucked his parachute and helmet and headed off into the jungle, his only choice of direction being away.

Before Larry knew it he was lost in deep jungle. He hoped that his trail was lost, too. He tried to remember what the intel types had told him about E and E or escape and evasion. He was supposed to follow some kind of natural feature or other. But what? He was concentrating so hard on remembering that he was three paces into knee-deep water before he knew his feet were wet.

"Oh, yeah," he said to himself. "A river. Follow a river. They should head south." He backed out of the water and started to crash through the underbrush next to the river.

"They also said something about a path. Maybe I should look for a path."

He found one a few yards away, a well-traveled one. He headed along it, making better and quieter time. He rounded a bend and took a couple of steps then suddenly pitched forward facedown. He lifted his head from the dirt. He felt a sharp pain in his chest. He reached down and pulled out the Buddha.

"I thought you were supposed to protect me from this kind of thing."

The Buddha just stared with its all-knowing smile. Then Larry glanced at the dirt just forward of his head. It didn't look right. He brushed it and found that dirt and leaves had been expertly strewn over a covering of thin branches. He lifted the branches to find a three-foot-deep hole across the path. Sharpened punji sticks embedded in the bottom of the hole pointed at his face.

"I guess I was supposed to avoid the paths instead of look for them."

He tucked the necklace back in his flight suit and tiptoed away from the path. "Sorry, little Buddha, I take it all back. You just keep doing what you're doing."

After what seemed like miles, Larry squatted under a giant tree. The undergrowth was dense near the roots and he figured he could take a protected break. He was about to doze off when suddenly the jungle began to dance. It was an explosion that just seemed to go on and on. It had started a couple of miles from him but it was growing in intensity. He grabbed the tree roots to hold himself in one place. The thunder kept getting closer. Finally his overtaxed brain told him what it was.

It was a Buff strike. A flight of B-52s, dropping tons of bombs in a string. A string that was heading straight toward him. And he couldn't even let go of the tree long enough to kiss his ass good-bye.

When it seemed that he was doomed for sure, the line of bombs suddenly jinked to the west. He stared in amazement as the jungle to the side exploded, then pulled the little golden icon from his flight suit. He stared at it in wonder.

Larry had no way of knowing that the reason he wasn't dead was that the bombardier on the last B-52 had made a serious mistake in his target coordinates, thereby saving Larry's life probably at the expense of his career. However, even the bombardier didn't know that his mistake had destroyed the majority of the target that the Army had requested be struck. The Army would therefore recommend that the young man be decorated at the same time that the Air Force would be trying to hang him. It was that kind of war.

Meanwhile back in the jungle, Larry had just about recovered the use of his ears and his legs. And he knew roughly where he was. Their squadron had been warned about the impending Buff strike. Intel had found out about a concentration of VC who were massing to penetrate the Thai border. That was good news and bad news for Larry. It meant that he was near the border to friendly territory. But he was there at the worst possible time, right at rush hour for the bad guys.

Then he heard it. Movement. A lot of it. Near him. It sounded like a large group of people moving through the jungle. Larry didn't know whether to run or hide. So, being Larry, he tried to do them both at once. He took off running while looking left and right for a place to hide. He ran right into a solid object and sat down suddenly. He looked up to see what he had hit this time, and stared into the eyes of a short man. A short man wearing the latest in basic black. A short man with a very big gun. The man was as startled as Larry. He quickly recovered and pointed his rifle at Larry's head while he called out in another language. Larry was rapidly surrounded by several more short men, all with very big guns. They all seemed to be very excited about Larry. They gestured for him to do something. He didn't know exactly what they wanted him to do but he could tell that if he didn't do it immediately, they would all shoot him with their big guns. Larry smiled and raised his hands. This was not what they wanted him to do. The leader raised his gun to fire at a stunned and uncomprehending Larry. Larry closed his eyes tight and waited for death. When it didn't come, he squinted one eye open.

The leader had lowered his gun and was staring at Larry's chest. Larry looked down. The VC was looking at the Buddha. After a minute of intense scrutiny, the leader said something to his companions. Larry watched as they all filed by to look at the Buddha. After only a cursory look they each faded into the jungle. The leader looked for a minute longer, then raised his eyes to Larry's. He shook his head in disgust and followed his men into the jungle.

After a couple of minutes Larry was able to get his mouth

closed again. He had ceased to marvel at his luck. He jumped to his feet, and started running in the direction opposite to the one that the VC had taken. He rounded a tree and skidded to a halt in horror. He was face-to-face with a demented demon. He heard a ting and glanced down. The biggest knife he had ever seen had just glanced off the Buddha and sliced through the chain like it was butter. Larry fainted.

He came to as the result of a couple of sharp slaps to his cheeks. The demon was standing over him. It grinned.

"Lieutenant, you must be the luckiest man in the world."

The demon introduced himself. He was an Army special forces major. The demonic mask was camouflage paint intended to break up the planes of the face and scare the daylights out of young Air Force types.

"We did not come here to rescue you. We've been tracking that squad of gooks. They're a nasty bunch. Their job is to sneak around and kill any villagers that they think are too friendly with us. They just wiped out an entire village. We saw them grab you but couldn't do anything about it. Our orders are to watch them, not fight them."

"Come on, let's get you out of here." The major pulled Larry to his feet. "Unless you want to spend some more time running around in the jungle.

As they moved out, the major looked back at Larry.

"Why did they let you go, do you think?"

"Probably because of my Bu . . ." Larry reached for his necklace to show the major. It was gone. The major's knife had cut the chain, and now the little number one Buddha was lost forever in the dense jungle undergrowth.

"Probably because of my natural good luck," Larry finished the sentence.

The special forces team was still confused after delivering

Larry to his unit. He had tripped over, run into, and crashed into everything and everyone in that section of Southeast Asia.

As Larry waved from the door (and slammed his hand against a metal fitting) of the aircraft sent to return him to the flying base, he saw the major shake his head in disbelief. He knew what the major was thinking.

He was thinking, *Now I know for sure what they mean by Dumb Luck.*

And somewhere, in a hidden patch of jungle, an exhausted little gold idol was settling in for a much-needed rest.

STUDENT GHOST

*U*NTIL *I went to live and work at a pilot training base I never imagined the impact of the training. We used to laugh about what we called students' disease. It seemed like the studs couldn't walk down stairs without an instructor to tell them how. Many times we'd see a student walk right in front of a car without even noticing. It was just that they were totally and completely focused on the instruction. It became the most important thing in their lives. It became life itself. Those who succeeded got wings. Those who failed lost a part of themselves. Some refused to acknowledge failure regardless of the evidence.*

An Air Force base has a feeling, a flavor. It is the basic character of the place and it's usually more intense than any civilian arena. Sometimes it takes a while to gauge the character of a base. You have to walk around, join in, be a member before you can taste the flavor. It's usually a gradual thing. Nothing really hits you in the face. It develops over time.

It has to do with the goal of the base, the reason that the base is there. It has to do with the people who work there and pursue that goal. It has to do with direction and guidance or, in some cases, the lack of it. It's usually pervasive, camouflaged by business as usual. But it is persuasive also. By the time you can touch it and taste it and define it, you're part of it.

It wasn't that way at Williams Air Force Base in Arizona. The guiding force at Willy grabbed you by the neck and dragged you in the minute you crossed the fence. It pulled you directly to the flight line and wrapped its arm around your shoulder and pointed with pride to the noisy ramp and said loud and clear, "Here We Train Pilots!"

Everyone on the base was caught up in the mission and goal of the base. They all trained pilots. Willy boasted the best weather, the best instructors, the biggest student load, the busiest ramp, and the most-crowded skies of any base in the world. It was kind of the big-mouthed Texas of Air Force bases.

With three runways and a huge ramp, the air traffic never stopped. Unlike most fields, where an approach to the main runway could be discontinued anywhere, if you were established on final ten miles from the main runway at Willy, you were either going to fly over the runway or land. There was no place else to go. Hopefully, if you chose to land, it would be on the runway. But that wasn't always a given.

Pilot training at Willy was known as the "year of fifty-one weeks." The base had only fifty-one weeks to turn a ground pounder into a flyer. The base also had roughly fifty-three weeks of training built into the syllabus. So somewhere along the way they crammed in those extra two weeks.

The students referred to it more as the day of twenty-seven hours. Pilot training was grueling. There was no time to relax or digest what was being taught. Classroom academics were taught in a style known as the Guillotine Method. Every day in every class you were required to put it on the line. You had to prove yourself worthy to hold the title of pilot. Each day brought more tests. And the tests were handled in a unique fashion. No open book, true-false, multiple guess with plenty of time to think. These were on your feet in your face interrogation tests with lots of derision and sarcasm to help you along. The instructors were not the kind and gentle old "Mr. Chips" type. They evolved more from the teaching techniques of Attila the Hun. Torquemada would have been pleased to know that the Spanish Inquisition lived on in the hearts and minds of flight instructors.

The Instructor

"I taught academics at Willy—several different classes. I know what kind of pressure is generated and I firmly believe in this method of teaching. I mean, we were trying to teach pilots here. We had to ensure that they knew the airplane and everything about flying it. They couldn't hesitate. They couldn't wait for something to come back to them. They had to know it cold, or somebody would die.

It was in one of my classrooms that I saw him. I was sitting at my desk between classes trying to catch up on some reading. I heard the door open and a chair move and I assumed it was one of my students getting in a little early. After a couple of minutes I looked up. Sure enough there was a stud in the back row, with his head down buried in a book. We referred to the students as studs. They thought it meant that they were macho types. We actually meant they were as dumb as a bunch of nails.

It was quite normal for studs to get to class early and try to learn everything they were supposed to know in five or ten minutes. It never works. I made it a point to pick on them.

I went back to my reading. A few minutes passed when I heard him say, "Sir, could you explain something to me?" I finished the paragraph I was reading and looked up ready to answer his question. He wasn't there. Nobody was there.

I didn't hear anyone open the door to leave. That was strange because it was a creaky old door. And there was absolutely no place to hide in the classroom. Believe me I've made students want to hide.

I got up and checked the hallway. It was empty. Not a soul. It was on my way back to my desk that I recognized the voice. I knew it couldn't have been him, but it was his voice. It was only frightening in retrospect.

I wish I knew what he wanted me to explain.

Flight training at a training base is just as difficult and serious as the academic training. It isn't a lot of graceful surly bonds slipping as the poet would have us believe. It is flying with all the fun carefully removed.

It starts at preflight. The airplanes used for pilot training are modern, capable jet aircraft. There are attack versions of both the initial and the advanced jet trainers. But to the Air Training Command the aircraft are training aids. And the students tend to think of them as booby traps.

The student arrives at his aircraft and is required to perform a very thorough inspection of every aspect of his appointed beast under the watchful eye of his instructor. He must be able to explain just what he is looking for and how everything should be set, positioned, or adjusted prior to starting engines. And woe to the student who misses something.

The Air Force tries to instill in the pilot the need for a very complete understanding of how everything must be so that an airplane will fly. They believe in using the carrot-and-stick technique of instruction without the carrot.

The Crew Chief

"I saw it, or him, on the flight line. I'm a crew chief for T-38s. I was catching a ride with the ramp tramp out to the bird I was supposed to preflight for an early morning go. It was way out on the end of the line. I was thinking I would get there early when all of a sudden the driver says, 'Looks like you're late again.'

I looked down at the end of the line and sure enough there's this student already checking the plane over. I looked at my schedule again thinking I must have read it wrong. According to it I still had a half hour before anyone was supposed to show up.

I watched the stud check the tail of the 38 as we pulled up to the parking stub. I jumped out and ran up and grabbed the forms. The student had disappeared around the tail so I went the other way around to catch up with him and find out why he was there so early.

He wasn't there. He wasn't anywhere on that side of the

aircraft. I looked under to see if I could see his feet on the other side. I thought maybe he had doubled back on me. He wasn't on the other side either. And he wasn't up in the cockpit. He wasn't anywhere. He was just gone.

The crew showed up at the plane right on time but I was so busy trying to find that other guy that I hadn't even started the preflight. The instructor chewed on me some for that.

I saw him out here a couple more times but I never got close to him. I know some of the other crew chiefs saw him too, but they don't like to talk about it much."

Flying aircraft, especially high-performance jet flying, is inherently a dangerous business. It's even more so at a training base. Students find out early that they must do every task exactly right every time if they want to survive. And even if they do everything exactly right, sometimes the aircraft won't cooperate. It is at that moment that the students take their most difficult tests. They find out if they have really learned the material about the airplane and flying it. They find out the hard way. And inevitably some fail their tests. And they aren't the kind of tests that you get to retake.

Air-training bases see more accidents than most bases. Instructors try their best to accident-proof their students, but it just isn't possible. The unofficial motto at Willy was, "in an operation of this size, you expect to lose a few." So it's a common thing. It's expected. But no one ever gets used to it.

The Student

"Yeah, I've heard the stories. I knew a lot of the guys who

told them, too. They were all sterling gentlemen and I'd never call any of them liars.

I myself have never seen a ghost stalking the flight line or whatever. But I did see something pretty strange. I saw it twice in fact. Blew my mind both times. Almost caused me to pink a ride. A pink is a deficiency on a flight mission. I guess somewhere back in the deep dark past they were printed on pink paper or something. Anyway, it doesn't matter what color they are. Students don't want any of them. You get more than one and you have to start looking around for a desk job.

Let me go back a little ways first. It was when I just checked into the program. They hit you hard and fast at first and I was walking around in a daze most of the time except I didn't have much time to walk around. One night around nine or ten o'clock a friend of mine who works in the tower gave me a call. He said that a stud in a T-38 just bought the farm. Ran right into a mountain.

I headed out to the base to see what was going on. Wanted to make sure it wasn't somebody I knew. It took me twenty minutes to get to the flight line and even after all that time I could still see where the accident happened. It was in the middle of a sheer face in the Superstitions. The fire was still burning brightly. A good share of the 38 is made out of magnesium. The plane was literally melting down the face of the cliff. He must have been busting the Mach when he hit that mountain.

Turns out I didn't know him but I'd heard of him. Had a reputation for flying with his head in the cockpit all the time. Trusting the instruments too much. He became object lesson number one for situational awareness.

Anyway, almost a year later, I was finally solo in a T-38.

It was a night mission. I was flying in the local area when suddenly I saw the whole side of the mountain light up. It was right where the other guy hit but I didn't remember that until later. I called RAPCON but they said that everyone was accounted for. I made a quick 180-degree turn to take a closer look. But it was gone. I almost flew out of my area trying to look for it. The instructor in the mobile tower saw the sloppy turn I made and started yelling at me. I was just barely able to lie my way out of it. I remembered the accident later in the club.

I saw it one more time when I was dual with an instructor. I pointed it out to him. He glanced at it and I know he saw it but he just told me to keep my mind on what I was doing. He didn't mention it after the flight and I didn't either."

When an aircraft goes down at a military base, the emergency team swings into action. The Air Force has some of the best-equipped, best-trained, and unfortunately, most-experienced rescue workers in the world. And those at pilot-training bases tend to be the best of the best. It's almost like the experience gained in a war.

During a war the pilots are often hampered in their attempts to return to base by battle-damaged aircraft. At a pilot-training base the aircraft are often hampered by the inability of the novice pilot behind the controls. Whatever the reason, all the personnel charged with the safe operation of the airfield have definite jobs to perform during an emergency. And those personnel at a pilot-training base have seen so many types and colors of emergencies that they know what to do immediately.

The Controller

"I never saw the ghost or whatever at Willy but the more I think about it the more I'm sure I talked to him. It was during an accident response. I was working the mid shift on a Wednesday night in the tower and we got a call from the radar guys that they had lost contact with one of the students. The bad thing was that they didn't know which one. It was never simple at a training base.

Anyway what happened was that it was a nice clear night and some of the students were going visual flight rules or VFR. They would just pop up and talk to radar when they wanted an approach. The pattern controller said some guy popped up and asked for vectors for a ground-controlled radar approach to the main runway. The controller identified his target and gave him a turn to the radar pattern, then asked for him to say his call sign. It had been garbled on first call-up. All the pop-up said was, 'Oh, shit,' and then stopped talking.

That was enough to get the controller's attention because swearing on the radio is a definite no-no. But then the radar target disappeared right after so he called us real fast. I checked with the super and he said to start a comm search. In a comm search everyone who is in the airport traffic area is supposed to give his call sign and location. As each one calls in the controller checks him off on the active flight progress board and makes sure everyone is accounted for.

I was taking the calls and rogering all the studs as they checked in. I was keeping a running count of the numbers because I knew we had twenty-seven airborne that night. We got calls from twenty-seven different aircraft and I thought everything was okay. But the ground controller said that there was a mistake because one of the call signs was wrong.

I asked her which one was wrong and which one was still missing. I thought maybe one of the studs had mixed up his call sign. It happens. I made a call for both of them to report in to the tower. The one who supposedly had the wrong call sign answered up but the other one failed to answer.

About that time things really went into afterburner. An instructor in a T-38 reported a fire on the ground about seven miles out on final. We scrambled the rescue helicopter and he beat it out reverse course to check it out. In the meantime we closed the center runway, which led to an emergency situation in itself. The wing king ordered all aircraft back to the ground.

They found the guy who didn't answer his call sign in the comm check. He was walking back to base after jettisoning the aircraft in some farmer's field.

It was about then that the senior controller pointed out what was wrong with the bad call sign. It was one we hadn't used in almost a year. None of the present-day students would have even heard it.

It wasn't until later at the club over a cold one that we got to talking about it. I'm almost sure that the call sign we heard that night was the same one the guy was using the night he plowed into the mountain.

Wonder what would have happened if I had cleared him to land?"

At a pilot-training base the students are introduced to another time-honored tradition of the Air Force. Since men first learned to fly they have maintained the tradition of the post flight. This post flight is usually carried out in a darkened, cozy room filled with similarly inclined fellow aviators. The room can come in many shapes and sizes, but it must be equipped with a friendly resident serving large quantities of soothing libation. Said libation must be of sufficient potency to ensure that the celebrants can wind down from the rigors of their flying.

Such places in the Air Force are never referred to as bars or saloons. Never anything so crass. They are dubbed "clubs" and are distinguished from bars and saloons primarily by their name.

A club on a pilot-training base can be a dangerous place for the uninitiated. It's hard for an outsider to understand how a group of people can get so wound up trying to wind down. Another danger in these places is the preponderance of hand flying going on. A pilot can get so caught up using both hands to demonstrate that impossible feat he just performed in his air machine, that he becomes a danger to himself and to innocent bystanders.

Suffice it to say that pilots never tire of trying to describe that undescribable experience of controlling a mechanical device through the air. Every club on every pilot-training base has a sign that says "Airplane Spoken Here."

The Bartender

"Oh yeah he was around the club all the time. At first it gave me the shakes something fierce. After a while I sort of got used to it. Sort of.

We first noticed it when the bell would ring. We had this bell at the end of the bar. If a student walked in wearing his hat or did something else he wasn't supposed to do, like forget his manners, one of his friends would ring the bell. Then the perpetrator would have to buy a round for the whole bar, whoever was there at the time. As soon as the bell went off, me or one of the other bartenders would make a quick count of the room to see how bad the poor fool would get nicked. We made it a rule that we only served beer on the bell. Some of those studs screwed up so often that anything else would have broke 'em.

Well, every time we had a bell round on a Wednesday night we'd end up with one too many beers. Not that somebody wouldn't volunteer to drink the extra. But we didn't want to charge the guy for any more than he should have to pay. It happened so regular that finally we started automatically subtracting one beer. But only on Wednesdays. We said to remember to subtract one beer for the ghost. Nobody complained.

That wasn't bad. Nobody actually saw the ghost or knew they saw the ghost anyway. But two or three times when we were closing up, one of the barmaids would see him. They didn't know who it was at first. One girl came up to me and said, 'I thought you threw out all the officers. There's one sitting at the corner of the bar nursing a drink.'

So, I went in to tell him we were closed. Wasn't anybody there. I looked all over, really searched the place, thinking he might have headed for the john and passed out or something. After searching the joint for the third Wednesday in a row I gave up. I figured out who he was, but I didn't tell the girls. Didn't want to scare them.

But I did ask them what he looked like. They all agreed that he looked like any normal second lieutenant student pilot. But they said he looked like a student pilot who just pinked a ride and was worried about making it through the program.

Wonder if any of those guys ever noticed when he joined them on Wednesday night. They were usually so jazzed up that even if they did know they were talking to a ghost, they probably would have just gone right on hand flying at Mach one."

Williams Air Force Base is closed now, the drastic need for military pilots reduced by the demise of the cold war. The runways that were so busy and so crucial to the activities of the base are just silent strips of useless concrete.

The pilots who learned their trade at Willy are spread throughout the world flying fighters and tankers and bombers and yes, airliners, with a consummate skill learned from the best of aviation classrooms.

But on a cold, dark desert night if you listen carefully you can just make out the whine of the power cart and the roar of twin jet engines. You might catch a glimpse of red and green wingtip lights as a white shape soars from the deserted field. He's up there trying again. Maybe this time he can get it right. Maybe this time he'll demonstrate his mastery of the air.

Maybe this time he'll earn his wings.

HISTORY LESSON

I WAS *proud of my uniform. Still am. I've been to places where civilians felt the same way I did about wearing the uniform. And I've been places where people hated me because I was inside the uniform. I've even been to places where just wearing the uniform was dangerous. But I've been to only one place where I'll never wear a uniform or carry a weapon again.*

"Son of a bitch!"

"What's wrong with it?"

"It won't run."

"Great. Wonderful. You just spent twenty minutes under the hood of this beast and all you can tell me is that it won't run? I know it won't run. That's why I called you in the first place. I'm stuck here in the middle of wherever this is with a truck full of pissed-off sky cops and the 'expert' from the motor pool tells me that the problem is that the truck won't run. Sarge, are you sure you were never an officer?"

The burly sergeant slid out from under the hood of the diesel vehicle and regarded the questioner with a sneer in his eyes.

"Keep your insults to yourself, Jensen. What I'm trying to tell you is that for the last twenty-two minutes I have gone over every system that makes this piece of crap a truck. I have checked every nook and cranny of this United States Air Force, one-each vehicle, type truck, and everything checks out according to book and checklist. And I have come to the considered conclusion based on many years of experience and skill. There is only one thing wrong with this truck."

"And what is that?"

"It . . . won't . . . run."

"Whatdaya mean . . ."

"What I mean is," the master mechanic interrupted the flustered driver. "What I mean is that the only thing wrong is it won't run. Everything else is fine. It should run. According to the laws of physics, mechanics, and sophisticated engineering, that engine should be purring along at two hundred decibels. I can't find a thing wrong."

"Maybe you didn't look hard enough. Maybe you missed something."

"Missed what?" The large NCO wiped the grease from his hands in a manner that indicated his disdain.

"I don't know . . . the carburetor or the belts . . . or that other gizmo, that what's-it."

"Look, Jensen, trust me. I didn't miss anything. I didn't miss the carburetor, or the wiring, or even the what's-it. I didn't miss it now and I didn't miss it the last two times we hauled this beast to the shop. There's nothing wrong with it."

"There's got to be something. And it was only one other time. There's just got to be something wrong. I don't know engines too well but I know that they don't just stop in the middle of the street in some deserted little pissant town for no reason."

"Well, you're right about one thing, Jensen."

"Yeah, I knew I was right."

The huge sergeant pulled the stub of a black cigar from his mouth and leaned his face in close to the other man.

"You're right that you don't know shit about engines. And what do you mean one time. I dragged your ass back to the base at least twice."

"Yeah, yeah, twice." The nervous driver backed away from the mechanic.

"But only one other time with this truck. The first time was another truck."

Sergeant Washington stopped. He backed away from Jensen and crossed his arms over his massive chest. He cocked his head to the right and regarded the driver with new interest. It was like he was taking the smaller man seriously for the first time.

"Are you sure it was another truck?"

"Yeah, yeah, another truck. This is five-zero. The first time it was five-eight. Check your own logbooks if you don't believe me. But I remember distinctly that it was five-eight the first time. We don't always get to drive the same truck, ya know."

The big mechanic said nothing but continued to stare at the driver. The intensity of his contemplation of the smaller man had an immediate effect.

"I ain't shittin' ya, Sarge. It was another truck."

Washington started. It was as if he suddenly became aware of the effect he was having on the driver.

"Don't worry, Jensen. I believe you. It was two different trucks I hauled out of the wilderness."

He turned and walked a short distance from the other man toward the back of the diesel truck.

"But what does that mean?"

"What do you mean what?" Jensen was confused by the question.

"What I mean is what is going on? Have I got the start of an epidemic? Are the trucks getting sick or something? I mean I just can't keep hauling in perfectly good trucks. Somebody's going to get a little suspicious. And before you know it I'll have a bunch of 'zeros' looking over my shoulder and giving me advice."

Both men grimaced at the thought of a lot of help from zeros, or officers, as the Air Force preferred to designate them.

"Well, I won't find out anything standing here in the middle of this beautiful village." His inflection turned the description of their location into surgical sarcasm.

"I guess I'll get on the horn and call the Hook."

"After you make your call, would you mind briefing the troops. I think they're getting tired of hearing bad news from me. And they all got guns."

The big sergeant nodded his head as he walked back to his radio-equipped vehicle to call for the wrecker.

"Motor pool dispatch, this is Charlie One."

"Charlie One, this is dispatch. Go ahead."

The speaker mounted under the dash of the blue pickup

crackled to life almost before Washington released the button on his microphone.

"Dispatch, see if you can get Hook up on this freq. I got a job for him."

"I'm here, Sarge. Your wish is my command." The response was wrapped in a higher-pitched carrier wave, indicating a different radio.

"That you, Hook?"

"You got me, Sergeant Washington. Whatcha got?"

"I got a sick troop truck on its way back from Lion Nine. Going to need a drag back to the base. And don't doddle getting out here. It's full of unhappy Sky Cops."

"Ten-four, Sarge. I'm on my way. Usual place?"

"I don't know what you mean by the usual place, but we're stuck in the middle of the booming metropolis of . . ."

Washington released the pressure on the mike button and glanced around, looking for a sign to tell him where he was.

"Don't tell me. Let me guess. I'll bet you're on the main drag of the town of Targa."

"I guess that's what they call this burg. But how did you know?"

"I'm always picking up dead vehicles from that place. Usually on their way to or from Lion Nine."

Washington stared at the radio for a minute, at a loss for words. Finally he keyed the mike.

"Just get your mass out here, Hook. Don't mess around."

"Ten-four, Sarge. I'm on my way. Out."

Washington clipped the mike into its holder and walked slowly back to the disabled diesel. He was trying to make some sense of the information that Hook had casually passed to him. He was determined to check a whole bunch of repair records as soon as he got back to the shop. Something was going on that he didn't understand. And that was a rare occurrence for Senior Master Sergeant Damien T. Washington. When it came to anything mechanical, there were no secrets. It was a matter of physical law. There was a reason for everything an engine did. All it took was a decent knowledge of the way things worked and enough time and any problem could be solved.

Washington thought of several ways to attack the problems. That's all they were: problems. Not mysteries—problems. He was thinking so hard that he walked past the rear end of the truck and almost got to the cab before he remembered. He had promised Jensen he would talk to the passengers. He reversed course and headed for the back door of the vehicle. He wasn't looking forward to explaining mechanical difficulties to a bunch of cops anxious to get out of the field.

The canvas flap that formed the back door of the converted cargo bed was pinned up to allow air circulation in the cramped quarters. Washington hauled himself up over the tailgate and dropped into the isle of the crowded compartment. The first thing that hit him was the silence.

When civilians think of the military, they usually envision camouflage-suited warriors armed to the teeth with the latest automatic instruments of death and destruction. But the steely-eyed killer is hard to find in the modern Air Force. The last bastion of the rugged GI in the Air Force is probably the Security Police department. Security Police, or Sky Cops as they are known by their fellow airmen, are assigned the task of guarding the most dangerous and advanced weapons systems in the military. They are trained in all the arts of deadly warfare and are the most disciplined bunch in the Air Force. Anyone attempting to enter a facility guarded by Sky Cops can attest to their utter lack of a sense of humor.

Sergeant Washington stood between the ranks of combat-ready troops and attempted to gauge the emotion he was receiving from all sides. It took him a while to get it. It took him even longer to believe. Washington stood in the midst of the toughest, best-trained, best-equipped fighters the Air Force had to offer. And from every one of them he caught the unmistakable indication of . . . fear. Washington was amazed. They sat in silence, staring straight ahead, radiating abject terror.

He cleared his throat. "Uh . . . who's in charge here?"

Washington barely heard the reply. It sounded more like a growl than speech.

"What's that?"

"I said when are we leaving?" the voice rumbled more distinctly. It still had the guttural quality of an animal sound.

"Are you in charge here?" Washington directed his question to where he thought the voice came from.

"No, I am," a man next to the sergeant answered without looking up from the floor.

Washington stared at the young NCO for a minute. Finally he decided on the safest course of action.

"Sarge, why don't you step outside with me and I'll explain the situation to you."

It was couched in the friendliest of terms, but it was an order none the less. Even so the young staff sergeant was obviously reluctant to leave the safety of the truck.

"Look, Sarge, this vehicle is inoperative and not repairable in the field. I have already alerted the tow vehicle and he's on the way. He should be here shortly to give you and your men a tow back to the base. I know your guys are anxious to get back and start their breaks. We'll get you out of here just as soon as possible."

Washington tried to look into the younger man's eyes as he explained. He was trying to find out what was wrong. But the man avoided his gaze absolutely. He was just as afraid as his men. He nodded understanding without a word. When it was apparent that Washington could think of nothing more to say, he turned and reboarded the troop truck in silence.

Washington was still perplexed as he sat in the cab of the giant tow vehicle sent to retrieve the diesel. Hook, the driver, was completing some required paperwork.

"Just about finished, Sarge." The grizzled redhead smiled up from his concentration on the printed form. "Can't pull a thing until the weight of the paperwork is equal to or greater than the weight of the load."

The sergeant smiled at the all-too-true observation. "Hook" was a character, one of the few tolerated by the modern Air Force. He was tolerated because he was not replaceable. He could drive anything and everything that had an engine and wheels. It was a widely held consensus that Hook could probably fly most of the airplanes in the Force. It was just that he considered flying a waste of time. So most of the brass put up with his nonmilitary bearing and his idiosyncrasies. And he was kept away from those who wouldn't understand.

"Hook, did you get a good look at the passengers?"

"Yeah, I saw 'em. Never get over all them teenagers with guns."

"But did you see how scared they were? What do you think is bugging them?"

"Oh, they're always like that when I drag 'em out of Targa. Been talking to the farmers, I suspect. Them old geezers love to scare the bejesus out of the kids."

"How? How do they scare them?"

"I reckon they been telling 'em about the witches."

Washington had been in the process of climbing down from the high cab of the tow rig. He almost fell from the next-to-last step.

"What do you mean witches?"

"Why the witches of Targa, Sarge." Hook waved his arm out the window of the truck in a sweeping gesture that took in most of the little town. "The place is lousy with 'em."

Sergeant Washington stood in the street and looked at the town for probably the first time. It was a strange place. Even the roar of the tow truck engine didn't disturb the eerie silence that shrouded the village.

"See ya back at base," Hook yelled over the noise of the vehicle. "Watch your ass, Sarge."

Washington stood by his vehicle in the sudden silence. There was not a soul visible in the little town. There were no children playing, no pedestrians, no curious onlookers. The town was not just empty, it was void. But the sergeant couldn't shake the feeling that he was being watched. Not just watched but studied, evaluated, examined.

"Witches, my ass," Washington scoffed. But then he fired up his engine and got his ass out of the town.

"It just doesn't make any sense." Washington was sitting at his dining room table surrounded by stacks of maintenance logs. He stared at the figures and shook his head in disbelief.

"This just doesn't make any sense at all."

"All right Senior Sergeant Washington, what doesn't make any sense?"

The sergeant jerked upright and turned to look at his wife, seated in her own circle of books on the couch. For a moment he just stared at her as if he couldn't quite place her. He had not been aware that he was speaking out loud.

"Oh, sorry, hon." He shook off his confusion. "Didn't mean to bother you. I know you're working hard correcting midterms. I'm just stumped by this data."

"That's all right, darling," said Gina, as she uncurled her long legs from under her. She stretched expansively as she stood. "I was looking for some excuse to tear me away from all this sophomore history, surprising as it can be. I honestly didn't know that the Fascists were an East LA rap group. What's your problem?"

Washington chuckled then turned serious once more as his wife draped her arm around his neck and looked over his shoulder at the scattered log forms.

"It just doesn't make any sense. I have twenty-eight breakdowns in the last three months. All of them break down at about the same place and all of them are unexplained by mechanical analysis. It's definitely significant, but significant of what."

Gina looked at the papers for a minute, then discovered an objection.

"They're not all unexplained. Look at this one. Cause: loose ignition wire. And this one says the problem was a broken fan belt."

"Gina those aren't the causes. Remember when I fixed your vacuum. I took it all apart and put it back together and it worked fine."

"Of course I remember." She smiled. "You're my little mechanical genius." She hugged his neck with some serious intent.

"Be that as it may, I did not fix the incredible sucking machine. I just took it apart, looked at it, and put it back together. But I couldn't tell you it fixed itself. Would've damaged my reputation." He ducked under her playful right cross and continued. "That's what my mechanics are telling me with these reports. Those findings were manufactured on paper because it's impossible to explain to the brass that a truck fixed itself."

"But twenty-eight trucks fixing themselves in a three-month period is impossible. It has to be something. And they all break down exactly halfway between the base and Lion Nine Missile Site. Right smack in the middle of Targa."

"Targa? Did you say they all break down in Targa?" Gina was suddenly wide-awake and very interested.

"Yeah, that's the place. Does that mean something to you?"

"No . . . well yes," she hesitated, obviously unsure how to continue.

"Well tell me. I'm ready to accept anything."

"It's just that this is pretty farfetched. The kids use Targa as some kind of spell or omen. They're always joking about it and scaring the younger kids with stories about that little town. And I know it's just high school kidding, but sometimes it sounds half-serious."

Washington frowned. "What are the jokes about?"

"About the witches . . . the witches of Targa."

"Actually Gina's students might have a point about the denizens of Targa. The town has quite a history for such a small place."

The speaker, Edward Tecter, was a rotund, jolly little man with white, flyaway hair. He looked like a casting director's idea of a history professor. His looks were perfect camouflage for one of the most incisive and knowledgeable historians in the country. He had come over to the Washingtons' house without hesitation at the mention of a mystery concerning Targa.

"Targa was actually settled in the early 1860s. It was built entirely by residents of a similar town in the Caucasus mountains. Their village, also called Targa, was located entirely in a pass in those mountains."

"To get to my point, and I will get to my point eventually, I'll have to tell you a little about those mountains." Professor Tecter even bumbled like a movie professor.

"The Caucasus were the traditional dividing line between Europe and Asia. This did not make the region an especially peaceful region in which to live. Conquering armies were constantly sweeping back and forth through the mountain passes, usually destroying everything in their way. This activity continued right up into relatively modern times. Many of the little pass towns and villages disappeared completely, beaten into the dust by the military hordes."

Gina couldn't contain her curiosity. "Is that what happened to Targa?"

"Quite the contrary." Edward smiled at the light of excitement burning in the eyes of his audience. This was his center stage.

"Targa was unique because it was never overrun. Invading armies and retreating hordes gave it a wide berth. This was unusual because of its position smack in the middle of a wide highway through the rugged mountains."

"Why would they do that? An army traditionally takes the path of least resistance."

"Why indeed, Sergeant Washington? I can't answer that. We have no clear answer to the avoidance of Targa by the armies of the world. Just rumor and innuendo. Scraps of or-

ders and scribblings remain. All make it clear that Targa was
to be avoided at all costs. They seemed to hint at supernatural fears, but they are as vague as they are serious. Only one
gives any cause for that military fear. Napoleon sent an order
to his commanders. It was an admonition not to forget the
witches of Targa. For they, and here I quote the exact text,
'for they will not abide the presence of warriors within the
boundaries of their town.' "

"Witches?" Sergeant Washington rose and walked from
the table to the fireplace as he contemplated this information.

"What did these witches do to the old-time armies, make
their horses vapor lock or something?"

The sergeant's feeble attempt at humor was disregarded by
the little professor.

"Oh, no, Sergeant Washington. If what little remains of
the history of old Targa is to be believed, then your people
have definitely been treated very generously indeed."

Tecter's eyes rose slowly to the ceiling as if in contemplation of the horror he had to relate.

"The stories talk of terrible battles, real bloodlettings that
filled the fields with bones. But they were battles of comrade
against comrade, brother against brother. For the only enemy
that the invading armies found were themselves. And they
fought. Fought amongst themselves with every weapon and
every bit of strength that they had. And to a man they died.
Only a few of the noncombatants, the camp followers, were
spared to whisper rumors of the terrible fate of armies foolish
enough to tempt the witches of Targa.

"Tell me, Sergeant," asked Dr. Tecter, returning to the
present. "Do the men you are pulling from the town ever
carry weapons? Do they carry modern weapons?"

"Yes, the latest." Washington's answer was slow in leaving his lips. He, too, was contemplating horror. But it was a future possible horror, not a remembrance of the past.

"Then, regardless of whether you believe in the rumors of witchcraft or not, I think it would be wise of you to choose another route for your troop movements. Patience is a temporary thing."

Washington nodded his head absently. He was trying to catch an idea that was ticking around his mind, just out of reach. Suddenly he sat bolt upright. Now he knew what it was he was trying to remember. A different type of troop movement was planned in the near future. A movement that would accompany one of the most feared weapons of all time. A nuclear tipped ICBM was to be moved to the base from Lion Nine. The route would take it right through Targa.

Sergeant Washington headed through the doors of the Security Police building almost at a run. He was determined to change the missile movement route. He just didn't know what he was going to use for an excuse.

As he walked down the main corridor, a familiar person walked out of an office. It took Washington a couple of beats to recognize the young Sky Cop commander he had pulled from Targa the day before.

Before he knew quite what he was doing himself, he grabbed the young man by the arm and pulled him into an empty lounge room.

"Hi Sergeant Washington. Sorry I didn't thank you properly for rescuing my troops when our truck a . . . broke down."

The young man seemed embarrassed by the memory.

"Forget it, kid. I just want you to be truthful with me. I think it might be very important."

The young man just nodded. He could see the older NCO was dead serious.

"What were you thinking, there in Targa? What were you feeling? I know you were afraid, I could feel that you all were afraid? But what were you afraid of?"

"Yeah, I was afraid. But I wasn't afraid of anything. I was afraid of myself; of what I would do if I didn't get out of that evil, fucking place."

Washington was surprised by the intensity of the reply, but he was smart enough to keep quiet and let the young man continue.

"You've got to understand, Sarge. My men mean everything to me. We trained together, we live together, we work together. We've been through some of the worst times you can imagine and come out great. We work together like fingers on the same hand. We trust each other. I probably know those guys better than I know my own brothers. And that's what makes it so scary.

"Yesterday, out in the middle of that stupid little town, I had the strongest feeling of . . . I don't know, it was kind of like claustrophobia. I felt that the longer I stayed there, the more I wanted to fight, had to fight. I wanted to slam a mag in my M-16 and shoot everything—and everyone—in sight. I just wanted to kill them all!"

"But there wasn't anyone there except your men."

The young man looked up and stared deep into the senior sergeant's eyes. Washington saw a look that he remembered from a long time ago and half a world away.

"Yeah, I know that," the young man whispered. "Didn't matter."

Sergeant Washington stood alone in the middle of the

street. He just looked. The town was just as deserted as it had been before. He looked at the empty streets, the empty buildings, the white, well-kept, and obviously empty church in the town square. He saw no one. But he felt the eyes.

When weapons and guards are moved by the Air Force they always take the most direct route. They always follow a straight line between Point A and Point B. Sergeant Washington knew that the brass did not believe in witches and such. But some of them had listened to him. Some had looked at his puzzling data and listened to his history lesson. And then they had talked to a security police officer who was no longer young.

And after that any straight line that the Air Force used to get from Point A to Point B did not, by definition, pass through the town of Targa.

A WAY TO GO

*I*N the heat of war it seems like there will never be
enough time to bury the dead, to memorialize them, to
thank them for their sacrifice, to even remember them.
But that time always comes sooner or later. It has to. It is
one of the few things that might eventually end war for all
time. But sometimes it takes a superhuman effort to get it accomplished.

Flying over, it was a very strange place. It was like a
child's toy, one of those magic pictures that changed as you
turned it from side to side. With the sun at one position, the
countryside looked green and solid, like some verdant valley
in South Carolina.

Then the angle of light would change and suddenly the
whole place looked like it was completely covered by water.

Square ponds of various predictable sizes, their boundaries defined by narrow earth dikes, monopolized the landscape from horizon to horizon. It went on like this for enough miles to be monotonous, then suddenly acres of dense jungle would grab his attention, and he would once again be entranced by the view.

Sandoval chuckled to himself. There it goes, putting on another mask. This place loves to fool me into thinking it's not really all that bad.

He had glided over the landscape countless other times and it always happened. He would forget where he was and the beauty of the place would grab him again. He would sit and stare and be totally caught up in the green world.

And then the helicopter would land and the door would slide open and the heat and smell of Vietnam would roll over him and he would remember once again that he was in hell.

It was the smell most of all that tore off the mask. Vietnam smelled bad. It was a sick, sour, dead smell. It was like nothing else. And because human memory is most effectively flagged and recalled by smells, Sandoval knew that this smell would forever be a precursor to nightmares.

But this time the door was still closed and the young lieutenant could sit back and enjoy his illusions for a while longer. They had a way to go before they got to the site. The crash site.

Jose Sandoval never once thought it strange that he was riding in a helicopter on his way to inspect the wreckage of another helicopter. Back in the world cops cruised to the scene of accidents in vehicles that mirrored participants: it was the same in 'Nam. The Hueys were the vehicle of choice in this war. They were the workhorses, the pack mules, and the all-purpose engines of destruction. Nothing special; they were just a way to get things done.

Jose was on his way to see one now. As an explosive ordinance disposal or EOD officer, one of his duties was to inspect the wreckage of aircraft equipped with his special toys. He had to see that the site inspection, rescue, and cleanup crews wouldn't be endangered by explosives. He was there to ensure the safety of the team.

Yeah, he thought. What about his own safety. Sandoval wasn't a superman by virtue of his specialist training. The only heightened sense he possessed was a very healthy respect for weapons of individual or mass destruction. Especially weapons that had been involved in aircraft accidents. Many of his lessons about dealing with the deadly stuff had come at a great expense. Quite a few of his friends had given their limbs or their lives demonstrating how not to dispose of weapons.

But this job wasn't going to be like that. This was going to be a piece of cake. Or maybe a waste of time was a more accurate description. Somebody had goofed. Jose wasn't really needed on this mop-up. Because the chopper they were going to see wasn't one of the armed-to-the-teeth birds of war. It was a slick—unarmed except for the M-60 door gun. Nobody left home without "the pig." It had been heading up-country to help move some noncombatants out of an area that was going red.

Jose snorted sarcastically when he thought of that description. At least three things were wrong with it. First, there was no such thing as noncombatants in this country. Everybody from the smallest child to the oldest grandpa, everybody was involved. They were born to it. He learned early that you "don't trust nobody." He learned that early enough to still be alive.

Second, "help move" was a government euphemism for forcibly relocate. The military didn't help anyone but themselves. It hadn't taken anyone long to learn that this was a no-win situation. No one was trying to win anymore; they were just trying to survive. Only the politicians thought something could be gained by being here.

Third, (and this was the kicker) Second Lieutenant Jose P. Sandoval did not need to be on this trip. That was what was tightening his jaw. There was no need for an EOD type to be sent out to disarm a slick. The only thing dangerous on that ship was the fifty-caliber from the M-60 gun. If the wreck had burned, most of that was probably all cooked off by now. If it hadn't, then the bullets would just lie around safe until somebody picked them up and stuck them in a gun. He didn't need to be here.

And that most of all sent a chill down his spine. Too many men bought it in this hellhole by being some place that they shouldn't have been. The irony was that everyone connected with this fiasco knew EOD wasn't needed on this job. But someone on the crew had fucked up. Someone had checked the wrong box on the flight plan. Someone, probably the copilot, had designated the copter a gunship. And now the paperwork showed that the crash involved aerial weapons. And if the paperwork said it, it must be so. And so they had to send EOD. Then their paperwork would match the wrong paperwork. In the military two wrongs did add up to be a right.

Jose couldn't blame the copilot. He made an honest mistake. He had just transferred from gunships. It was an automatic mistake. Probably his last one. There were no reported survivors of the crash.

"LZ coming up." The interphone in his helmet crackled to life, startling Sandoval out of his thoughts.

"Prepare to disembark. And thank you for flying the friendly skies of Vietnam."

Jose stared out the side window as the Huey slid closer to the ground and slithered over a ridge covered with trees. As they topped the ridge, he glimpsed a couple of primitive buildings over the next ridge. Then the pilot pushed the chopper back to the safety of the ground and he lost sight of the village. The helicopter swung around in a wide arc and Sandoval's attention was immediately riveted to a scorched area in the exact center of the valley.

The object sitting in the middle of the burned-out circle might have once been a helicopter; now it was hard to tell that it had been man-made. It looked like slag from a blast furnace. It looked small and black, lacking any recognizable form or shape. Most of all it looked dead. The metal, fiber, and electronics that had comprised this aerial vehicle were now all of a piece, all mixed and mingled and stirred by a terrible blaze. The raging inferno had left its individual parts indistinguishable from the whole.

Sandoval shuddered as he realized that the passengers were now part of that mass. Man and machine had been blended beyond recognition.

His helicopter thumped to the ground as if the pilot had suddenly stopped flying. There was a pause as everyone on the bird contemplated the center stage of the clearing. Then the door slid open and the stink and heat hit him in the face with a physical jolt. At first he thought the heat was radiating from the wreck, the smell coming from the death it held. But the sergeant tapped him on the knee and he broke from his reverie and realized it was just Vietnam. Just the normal heat and the normal smell of Vietnam.

"Area appears clear and safe." The banter was gone from the pilot's voice on the intercom. "Clear the ship. Give me a thumbs-up when you're all clear. I will dust off and return with the . . . with the KP team. Good luck."

Sandoval and the other two airmen watched from the tree line as their ride lifted vertically and sailed back over the ridge and out of sight. Soon even the sound of the engine was gone. Reluctantly the three men turned their attention back to the wreck.

Accompanying him on this worthless mission were two Sky Cops from the air base they had departed this morning. Air policemen are usually the only members of the Air Force trained for actual ground combat. Flyers, and ground pounders like Sandoval, were given cursory training with pistol and rifle. Usually just enough to teach them that they didn't want to carry a gun for a living. But the Sky Cops were as good a fighting force as produced by any army.

The two men, a tech sergeant named Rockford and a two-striper named Reagan, but called Junior, were considered enough to secure the perimeter of this operation. At least until the rest of the team rolled in on the next chopper.

They stood and stared at the mass of blackened metal. Sandoval thought of a line from some old movie. "What a magnificent catastrophe."

Sergeant Rockford was the first to break the silence.

"Orders, Lieutenant?"

"Yes . . ." Sandoval took a minute to clear his head of a whole host of nightmare possibilities.

"Well, let's play this farce by the book. This place looks

pretty secure, so let's sweep the area looking for unexpended ordinance. In the unlikely event that you actually find something, just leave it lie and mark the spot with a piece of paper."

"What about the vil?"

"What do you mean, Sarge?"

"The vil. On the other side of the ridge. Think maybe somebody ought to check it out?"

Jose contemplated it for a moment, then nodded his head in agreement.

"Yeah, you're right. Nobody said anything about a village in the mission brief. Guess we better be sure it's friendly."

Rockford dispatched the younger man with an admonition to look and listen and come back without exposing himself to danger. The airman seemed to agree with the plan wholeheartedly, especially the part about keeping his ass out of harm's way.

After the young man departed through the trees, the other two reluctantly returned to the task at hand.

A thorough search of the area produced nothing but a sense of sadness and despair. The pilot had apparently chosen the clearing when the trouble developed with his helicopter. It was chosen well. Maybe he had seen the village and wanted to avoid it. Maybe he felt the need to avoid useless danger to the inhabitants. Maybe he just felt the clearing had fewer obstacles to avoid. It would have been a perfect spot to land. It was just as perfect a spot to crash.

It looked as if the craft had come straight down from a considerable height. Helicopters were the only flying machines that could crash that way. And in this war they did just that with alarming regularity.

The wreckage pattern attested to very little if any forward

momentum. It also showed that the last landing was a hard one. Under the wreckage there was even a small crater caused by the impact.

Sandoval wondered about the wreck and the final minutes of the crew as he surveyed the site. Did the horrendous impact cause the fire or were they already burning before they hit? Did the crew know they were doomed or did they think they had a chance right up until the last minutes of their descent into hell?

His eyes swept the ground and the wreck as he contemplated the last minutes of four men. Suddenly his attention was riveted by an object in the wreck.

A hand shook his shoulder, then gently turned him away from the accident.

"Sir, I think the area is secure and safe."

"I agree, Sergeant." It took Sandoval a while before he could get the words out.

The only discernible structure left by the blaze was the frame that used to hold the pilot's side window. And perched on the edge of that window frame, Sandoval had seen a perfectly normal hand. It was encased in a flying glove that looked new and undamaged. It was just a hand, with a little of the lower arm. It looked perfectly normal except that it ended in a lump of charred and melted debris. At that moment, just before he turned away, a breeze came up and the smell of cooked meat wafted over him, locking the memory of the hand in his mind forever.

Darkness came to Vietnam like no other place. It seemed as if it was full daylight and then full nighttime with no remembered twilight. The stars and moon of the season gave a perpetual glow to the surrounding area. In the valley it would never be totally dark, not unless some sudden storm covered the sky brightness momentarily. It happened enough to be expected and prepared for but it really didn't seem to be a possibility on this bright night.

The three men were huddled together near a small fire under the tree canopy on the edge of the clearing. The fire was more for emotional comfort than for warmth and not a good practice in a war zone. But this didn't seem to be a serious part of any war zone and the fire was especially necessary.

Junior had returned from his survey of the nearby village. He had looked and listened and seen exactly nothing. It appeared to be empty. Whether the inhabitants had moved or were just away temporarily was of little consequence. Just so they were gone and, therefore, not a threat to the little party.

Junior had been on his way back to the clearing when his radio squawked to life and almost scared him to death. He had forgotten to turn it down when he went on his recon. Bad mistake. It was the type that could get you killed. It had scared him enough to be a good object lesson for the future.

The message had been terse. Their ride into and out of this place had landed at the air base and been grounded for maintenance. It might have been that the pilot, just returned from the last resting place of a sister ship, was being overly cautious. But whatever the reason or motivation, the fact was that no one would return for the group this night. They were on their own. As a final gesture of embarrassed guilt, the pilot had passed on the fact that their area was still green and not expected to go red.

The group was comforted by this news but still alert. Things changed rapidly in 'Nam.

Lieutenant Sandoval okayed the fire and set a watch

schedule, giving himself first watch. He contemplated the wreck over the last glowing embers of their campfire. He had thought it would be frightening to keep watch over a death scene at night. It wasn't. It was just sad: deep down mournfully sad.

"What the hell? Get away from there!"

Sandoval came fully awake at the shouted commands from the young airman.

"What is it, Junior?"

"Over there by the wreck, LT. By the right side. Can't you see it. It's a dink. Walking right up to the wreck. A lousy dink. Hey, get away from there!"

The last was shouted much too close to his ear. Sandoval grabbed the young man's arm to settle him as he allowed his eyes to adjust to the starlit darkness. He sighted the line Junior indicated with his outstretched arm. Finally he started to see something—movement at first, then form. The conical hat reflected enough starlight to be the first thing discernible.

"It looks like some old mama-san. But what's she doing out here?"

Rockford was awake. He had joined their contemplation of the scene.

"Junior, I thought you said the vil was empty." There was just enough accusation in his voice to turn the young man around.

"It was empty. Dead empty. I don't know where the hell she came from, Sarge, but it wasn't from the vil."

Before either of the senior men could protest, the young airman grabbed his M-16 and was across the clearing in three strides.

"You're not supposed to be here. This is government property."

The indignant boy grabbed the arm of the old villager and tugged her back. She turned and lifted her eyes to the tall young man. The moon illuminated her wrinkled face. The cold glow also illuminated the sorrow embedded in her furrowed countenance. All three men could see the sadness, could feel the pain.

The young man let go of the arm with a partially smothered gasp. Mild reproach crossed the ancient brow and then she turned back to the wreck.

"Let her be, Junior. I don't think she means any harm." Sergeant Rockford beckoned the younger man to return to their position.

"But Sarge, we can't let her mess around the crash."

"I don't think they intend to disturb the wreckage."

It took a minute for the multiple designation to sink in for Jose. He was startled to see that the old woman had been joined by three more of her kind. It was impossible to tell with any certainty in the weak light if the newcomers were as old, or even female. But a strong feeling that accompanied their silent arrival made the composition of the groups very clear.

All three Air Force men watched silently as the figures approached the blackened circle of earth that held the remains of the craft. They watched as the figures chose four separate points around the wreck, roughly approximating where the four members of the crew must have been when they died. They watched as the old ones silently bowed to the pile of ruined machinery, then in perfect unison sank to their knees.

From the kneeling group came a gentle sound. The sound was so light and low that it could almost be mistaken for the rustling of branches in the woods or the susurration of a nearby stream. But it wasn't.

"What is it, Sarge?" Sandoval was transfixed by the sight and sound.

Rockford was frowning at the sight in concentration. "I think it's a ceremony. I think they're Buddhists and this is something for the dead."

"You mean they're holding a funeral or something for our guys." Reagan was clearly confused by the thought.

"Not a funeral really. Buddhists don't think that way about death."

"How do you mean, Sarge?" whispered the lieutenant. None of the three realized how quietly they were talking. It just seemed the right thing to do.

"Near as I can understand, they don't have funerals like we do. They believe that death is a natural step. A step along to the next life that must be taken carefully. They don't believe in doctors and hospitals trying to prolong life. And they don't believe that dying people should be drugged up so they can't feel pain. They believe that you should exit this life meditating. The *Book of the Dead* gives specific instructions on how to die."

"The book of what?" Junior was still watching the scene around the wreckage, but he was listening intently to Rockford's explanation.

"The *Book of the Dead*. It's kind of a short course in death and dying. It's really more like a map for the faithful to follow into the next life. What those people down there are doing is helping the crew remember how to get on."

"But that crew is already dead. They were toast hours ago."

"Yeah, but the way they believe is that there's still time to help. The spirit or whatever is supposed to hang around for a while after death."

A mild shudder passed around the watchers as they contemplated this bit of information.

"They believe that they can set an example of the way to do it, the way to chant and meditate. Eventually the spirit will get the idea and join them. Then they can pass on to what comes next."

All three fell silent as they watched a group that they could barely see and listened to sounds they couldn't really hear.

"How will they know?"

The question retrieved their attention. The two older men turned to face the boy.

"How will they know when it's over? How will they know that it worked?"

"I don't know how but I guess they do." Sergeant Rockford gestured with his eyes back at the crash site; the other two turned and gazed in silent wonder. The crash site was empty. The mourners had departed as silently as they had come. It was as if they had faded like the ghosts they came to help.

The vibration through the floor was like a gentle hand shaking the three back to some semblance of alertness. The rest of the night at the site had been peaceful, uneventful, and anything but restful.

"You guys look like shit warmed over." The gunner laughed as he looked at the bedraggled trio. Then, remembering that one of the group was an officer, he added, "No offense LT."

Sandoval just shook his head without raising his eyes. The

night had faded from the sky but his questions had not faded with it.

"You guys didn't like being all alone with a bunch of dead guys, didya. Bet it gave you the shakes."

The gunner was intent on being obnoxious. It seemed to be a hobby with him. Only Junior was willing to rise to the bait.

"It wasn't so bad. And we weren't so lonely either."

"Yeah, I'll bet. Who kept you company? The bogeyman? Or maybe the Grim Reaper?" His braying laugh was just as obnoxious as the rest of him.

"Nah, just some old villagers." The airmen seemed reluctant to discuss what they had seen with a jackass like him.

"Villagers, my ass. What villagers? Not from that vil. Ain't nobody in that vil. Ain't never going to be nobody there ever."

"What do you mean Airman First Class Michaels?"

The use of his formal designation by the senior NCO sobered the gunner somewhat.

"That vil, Sarge, er . . . Sergeant Rockford. That's Chou Loc. You guys know about Chou Loc, don't you?"

The look in the eyes of his listeners gave the negative answer.

"Nobody lives in Chou Loc anymore. Charlie took care of that. Used to be a right friendly place. They really liked GIs there. Hated the commies, too. Helped us out a lot. Then somebody told the bad guys about it. Charlie marched a bunch of real bad dudes in there one night when the gunships were off protecting some other vil. The headman tried to get the word back to us, but by the time it got through all the politicians and dipshits, it was all over."

"What was all over?"

"They took care of Chou Loc." The obnoxious gunner warmed to his tale. "They decided to make it an example for all the other villages. First they started with the headman and his family. They made him watch while they used and abused his wife and daughter, then they killed them in front of him. Then they brought out all the little kids. They skinned 'em in front of their parents and the headman. Took 'em a long time to die. Next they killed off all the women and young men. Did it as slow and painful as they could. Finally they killed all the old folks, one at a time. Made a game out of it. I hear they really enjoyed their work. After it was all over they took the bodies and made a bonfire in a clearing outside of town. Didn't want to burn the vil. They wanted to leave that standing so that no one would forget what happens when you don't help Charlie. Hey, I'll bet that was about where you guys spent the night."

"How . . . how do you know all this?" Sandoval spat the words out. The gunner recoiled as if he had been accused of the atrocities.

"Hey LT, I'm just reporting what I heard."

"What the lieutenant means is how did you hear it in such detail, Airman?"

"That was the neat thing about it. They made the headman watch and then they turned him loose. Needed someone to tell the story. That's all he did after that. Just tell the story over and over. He was crazy as a loon after that. Real bughouse. Funny old geezer. But it worked. Nobody goes near that vil."

Sandoval shut out the laughter of the gunner and stared out the window of the speeding helicopter.

He was now certain about what had happened on the previous night. Some way, somehow, the three had witnessed the former inhabitants of Chou Loc. The villagers had been unable to take the proper steps into the next world. They had been parted from this one too suddenly. Just as suddenly as the crew from the helicopter. They had been unable to help their friends and family on the road. They had been unable to help themselves. So they helped whoever they could.

Sandoval looked out at the deceptive landscape sliding under the Huey. Maybe Vietnam wasn't hell. Maybe not. But you could sure see it from here.

ABOUT THE AUTHOR

Charles D. Hough was in the United States Air Force for twenty years. He started off his Air Force career as an air traffic controller and left with the rank of major. As an aviator, he amassed thousands of hours of flight time in various types of aircraft. After retiring from active duty, he went to work for a government contractor as a combat air crew trainer. He lives in North Dakota with his wife and two children.